THE GREEN-EYED PRINCE: A RETELLING OF THE FROG PRINCE

THE CLASSICAL KINGDOMS COLLECTION NOVELLAS, BOOK #1

BRITTANY FICHTER

WANT MORE OF YOUR FAVORITE FAIRY TALES?

If you would like to read more about your favorite characters (meaning FREE secret chapters and short stories), you can sign up for my no-spam email list.

Details at the end of this book.

To Michelle

Moving is always a lonely task, and out of all of our Air Force moves, this one was the hardest. Finding you, a fellow fairy tale fanatic sister-in-Christ, was such a gift from God. From letting me drag you to Beauty and the Beast to sharing my love for 50's style dresses to reading my books blindly, you've been such an inspiration and such a cheerleader, and I'm so grateful to have you as my friend. I love how you see the world outside of the box. Please don't ever change.

CHAPTER 1

ALL OF THEM

T here." Kartek gave the little girl's arm a quick squeeze and smiled. "You're ready to play Clump Ball again. Just be careful of the big boys this time. Sometimes they forget to look for brave little girls like you."

The girl gave Kartek a big toothy grin as her mother bowed. "I thank you, my jahira!" She patted her big belly. "I do not know what I would do without her." She smiled down at her daughter. "Sashi is my greatest help around the house now as we get ready for the baby."

Kartek nodded once. "May the Maker gift you a healthy, strong child and a safe delivery." She looked over at the line as the woman took her daughter and left. Before she called for the next in line, however, something to her left caught her eye. Careful not to appear alarmed, she waved over her bodyguard and nodded in the direction of the column of thick yellow smoke that was rising in the air.

"Ebo, what do you think that is?" she asked in a low voice.

Her bodyguard frowned. "No one knows. Fadil believes it is simply a brush fire, no closer than the river at most."

She frowned. True, a thunderstorm had moved through the valley the night before. Still, something bothered her, an uneasiness she couldn't quite put a name to. "The smoke is an odd color to be caused by a brush fire."

"Do you wish to cut this morning's healings short?" Oni, Kartek's favorite handmaiden, asked.

Kartek studied the smoke for another moment longer. Because of the high city walls, seeing its base location was impossible. Still, if there had been any real threat, Commander Fadil and Ebo would have swept her out of the public plaza long before. They had done it before during far less threatening situations. So she shook her head. "No, thank you. The line is short today. I will finish here as usual." She looked up at the line of people standing before her and put on her most reassuring smile. "Who is next?"

Truly, the line wasn't as long as it normally was. Sometimes, it wrapped so far around the pool and into the village that she had to move everyone back into the palace. She preferred to avoid healing inside, as having great numbers of citizens crowding about the throne room created more work for the palace staff. But the sun made it too hot to heal outside much after dawn, at least in the dry season. As there were only a dozen citizens still waiting their turn with her, however, she should be able to get through them all before the sun rose too high. So she dipped her hand in the water of the pool where she sat and rubbed it on her face.

A man approached her and bowed from the waist. "I thank you, Jahira, for seeing me."

"And what do you need healing for this morning?" she asked. He held out his hand, and Kartek leaned in closer to see the deep gash that ran across his palm. "How did you get this?"

"I was working in my garden when I tripped and fell on one of my tools."

Kartek nodded and reached for his hand. "Oni, a clean rag, please."

Her handmaiden handed her a rag, and Kartek dipped it into the jar of water beside her that Oni had brought for this very purpose. She held it over his palm and squeezed the water out so that it ran over the cut. Red water splashed onto the ground and the man clenched his jaw.

"I'm sorry for the pain," Kartek said as she laid the rag down and folded his hand gently into a fist. "But if I don't clean it, the healing won't be as thorough." Then, closing her eyes, she exhaled, letting the warmth run from her heart through her shoulders, down her arms, and into her fingers that held his. She heard him gasp, and she couldn't help smiling a bit. Though her eyes were closed, she could envision the familiar pink mist covering their hands.

It never ceased to amaze her, either.

"My jahira," Oni leaned in as the man thanked her profusely and the woman behind him came to the front of the line. "Seamstress needs to see you when you are finished."

Kartek's heart paused briefly before returning to its usual rhythm. "The wedding dress?"

Oni nodded, her brown eyes a little too bright with excitement.

Kartek sighed. "Very well. As soon as we are finished here." Suddenly, she was wishing the line of those waiting to be healed was far longer. No, that wouldn't do. She should be grateful that the Maker had kept her city safe from a great calamity or sickness through the night. Still, her gown fitting appointments hadn't held much allure for her since her parents had been—

No, she wasn't going to think about that, either.

The sun was peeking out from the barren craggy mountains in the distance as Kartek waved goodbye to her final subject and turned to go with Oni. Ebo hovered behind, too, of course, but that was nothing new. Kartek couldn't remember a time when Ebo hadn't hovered.

"You're nervous, aren't you?"

Kartek wanted to grimace at her friend's forward questions as they crossed the square toward the palace. But as she glanced up at Oni, however, a movement caught her eye. Kartek stopped walking and squinted.

"Did you see that?" Kartek asked, taking a few steps toward where the movement had been.

"No. Where?"

"There. At that back gate in the wall. The one the servants use to get to the fields."

Oni huffed and looked for a moment before shaking her head. "I see nothing. And do not try to change the subject. Every time we go to finalize more wedding details, you become less and less enthusiastic." She leaned in. "Are you nervous?"

Kartek stared at the now empty space where she had been sure she'd seen a face a moment before. The skin on her neck prickled. She considered going to Ebo, only to realize that her bodyguard was already on his way back from investigating. When he said nothing, though, she shook her head to herself and tried to pay attention to Oni once again.

"Well, are you?" Oni pressed.

Kartek pursed her lips as she considered how to answer. The jahira was never supposed to be nervous, or at least she was never supposed to show that she was anything less than perfectly at ease, a subject Ahmos had spent hours lecturing her about. But Oni knew her too well to be fooled, and they both knew it.

"I suppose it's beginning to seem more real," Kartek said, pitching her voice low.

"I should hope so!" Oni laughed. "You are to be married in a month! If you're not ready for it now, I don't know if you will ever be!" She grinned shamelessly. "I would be nervous. Your betrothed is so large and fearsome. Kissing him would be more like kissing a mountain than a man!"

"Oni!" Kartek hissed, trying to smother a giggle. "That is not an appropriate way to speak of the Rayis!" She glanced around as the palace doors swung open for them. "Or my future husband."

"It doesn't change anything." Oni smirked.

As if Kartek needed reminding. She hadn't seen her betrothed often, not more than twice a year since they'd been betrothed, but every time she saw Gahiji, he seemed to have grown in both muscles and height. Kartek tried to think of something else, but it was too late. She could already feel the red blush rise to her cheeks, which only made Oni laugh more.

The palace was already decidedly cooler than her spot at the pool had been, the six white open archways greeting her as she stepped inside. Servants scurried around. Music came from somewhere at the south end of the palace, and laughter was heard frequently as they moved up a set of spiraling sandstone steps, down one stone-laden hall, then another. As they walked and Oni continued to try and pull details out of Kartek, Kartek closed her eyes and drank in the tranquility of her home.

Compared to the castles of the north, particularly Destin's renowned Fortress, her sprawling palace was rather unprotected. Its wide entrance with its six arches and eight pillars opened up directly to the main city plaza, where their prized oasis pool sat, the heart of the city. Sandstone houses and shops surrounded the large plaza, which was nearly always filled with families shopping, vendors with carts, and curious travelers come to see the Jewel of the Desert, as the natural pool was often called. There were no moats, trenches, or even a gate to separate Kartek from her people. But really, with the wall that ran around the city, which stood three stories high and backed the palace courtyards directly, there had never been much reason to build the palace defenses any further. And Kartek was glad. Few of the windows even had glass, for this allowed the dry air to waft through the palace to keep it cool. Many of the inner palace walls were only fancy trellises for exactly the same purpose. King Rodrigue of Destin liked to grumble about how this left the palace vulnerable for attack, but Kartek felt the openness allowed the palace to feel far more welcoming to her people than any of the northern castles did. It also allowed her palace to feel like home.

Finally, they reached the seamstress's quarters. Kartek took a deep breath of the oils used to rub the clothing as they entered. She had loved this room as a child, with its neat stacks of fabrics that reached the ceiling, stacked wooden crates of dyes, and baskets of fastidiously organized needles, pins, and threads.

"Good morning, Jahira." Ipy bowed but fixed her sharp eyes on Oni as they walked in. "Oni, I thought I told you to have her here an hour ago."

"That is my fault," Kartek said. "I was healing at the pool this morning. I apologize for the delay. Now, let's begin."

Ipy appeared momentarily mollified, though her satisfaction rarely lasted very long with anyone, least of all Oni. She began directing her assistants to remove Kartek's clothes and put the wedding dress on for its final adjustments.

Kartek really couldn't see why they needed so many adjustments. The green gown seemed nearly as simple as her other dresses, thin so she wouldn't sweat to death in it during the ceremony or after during the feast. Its only real changes from her everyday clothes were the jewels that lined its edges. Pleats ran along the skirt's length, which reached just down to her ankles. Still, the swishing of cool cloth felt good on her skin as they folded and tucked and pinned, and Kartek closed her eyes and tried to picture the day she would actually wear this.

Preparations would begin early in the morning even though the ceremony wouldn't take place until after the sun set. She tried to imagine what it would feel like to have the soft green silk brush her legs as she walked toward Gahiji.

She didn't want to admit it, of course, but Oni had been right when she accused Kartek of being nervous. Not that Kartek didn't trust Gahiji, of course. Her parents had chosen him after looking at dozens of possible suitors. His match was the most obvious for political and military reasons. And though he came from a wild, nomadic people, there was nothing about him to suggest that he might not make a fine husband. Together, Kartek and Gahiji would unite Hedjet and the tribes to create a stronger people in the desert.

But at this very moment, politics were the last thing on Kartek's mind. All she could see in her head was him leaning down to kiss her, a giant of a man who dwarfed even her. And she was considered tall for a woman.

She shuddered.

"Are you well, Jahira?" Ipy paused in her work and looked up at Kartek.

Kartek opened her mouth to assure the woman that she was fine, but a knock sounded at the door. One of the seamstress's girls went to get it. After speaking for a moment with whomever was outside, she returned.

Ipy pulled a pin from her mouth and frowned at the girl. "What is the matter?"

"They say we need to look outside."

If the warble in her voice wasn't enough to put Kartek on edge, the way the girl's face had turned ashen was. Everyone ran to the windows and peered out. When she found her own place at the window, Kartek froze.

To the east, over dunes of glittering sand poured people. Hundreds of people. Like ants they marched forward, turning the dunes from gold to brown, gray, black, and whatever other colors they wore.

"Are they warriors?" one of the girls whispered.

"No," Oni shook her head. "There are women and children among them."

Kartek squinted against the bright reflection of the sand. No colors were carried to denote the tribe's identity. She tried to recall which of the ten tribes had so many people, but none came to mind.

"My jahira."

She turned at the sound of a man's voice. "Ahmos. Which tribe is it?"

Ahmos crossed his arms, the very picture of confidence, but she didn't miss the way he ground his jaw. "Not which tribe, Jahira." He paused and glanced at the women in the room. "It's all of them."

CHAPTER 2

BLOODLINES

A ll of them?" She stared blankly at him. "All ten?"

"Perhaps we might speak of this in private?"

She nodded. "Let me change. Quickly, Ipy."

Ahmos went back outside again as the women removed the wedding garments and Kartek donned her day clothes once again. She tried to ignore the shaking in her knees as she joined her head alder in the hall.

"Have all ten tribes ever come together before this?" Kartek racked her memory. "For something other than the wedding of a Rayis . . . or a funeral?"

Ahmos only raised his eyebrows.

Kartek closed her eyes and drew in a long, shuddering breath through her nose. How many times she had prayed nothing like this would ever happen, at least until she had been jahira for much, much longer. Healing she was comfortable with, mending accidents from scythes and falls, broken limbs and minor diseases. Meeting with stewards and local rulers to discuss kingdom finances and laws for the streets was manageable as well. Not easy, but still manageable. But this? Before she died, her parents had never given her a lesson on what to do when ten of the world's most fearsome tribes appeared outside one's city gates.

Kartek swallowed, her voice threatening to squeak. "War. Of course. What do you suggest we do?"

"As the presence of the families makes it unlikely that they're openly declaring war here and now, and very few of the warriors have been spotted, I suggest we attempt a civil discussion first."

"Shall I go out to them?"

He looked at her as though she were mad. "By yourself? Of course not!"

"Then you come with me."

He rubbed his shiny head. "The tribes respect strength. Any sign of weakness will do nothing but make them doubt your ability. They could easily interpret my presence as that of a chaperone rather than an adviser."

Kartek closed her eyes and groaned. "I am seventeen years, Ahmos. Hardly enough to command their respect on my own, no matter what I do."

Ahmos thought for a moment. "You are right. You must speak to them. About that we have no choice. But think. How can we enforce the idea that *you* are the one in charge, that you hold the upper hand?"

Kartek closed her eyes and rubbed the back of her neck. After a moment of thought, she opened her eyes again. "What if we invite them *here* to talk? No warriors, just the tribal heads. We can establish authority by announcing our requirements before they make their requests or demands or whatever they wish of us. In the meantime, we can give the families access to the outer springs and wells so that it makes us appear generous and in control."

Ahmos's mouth turned up nearly imperceptibly. "Now you are thinking like a jahira."

IN THE TIME it took to get the squabbling tribal heads assembled in one of the palace rooms, the time for the midday meal had passed and the sun had risen to its peak. Indignation and vexation at the tribes flared up again as Kartek stormed across the palace to meet them. What sane person walked great distances when the sun was up, let alone forced his people to cross the mountains and the dunes in such fearsome heat? The tribal heads had put their women, children, and elderly in great danger, and now *her* people were being forced to compensate for their foolishness.

Kartek kicked at a stray pebble, but it only served to crack one of her toenails.

To make everything worse, a foul stench had begun to fill the air, and it seemed to be coming from the still rising column of smoke in the distance. In the palace courtyard, the town plaza, even up inside her rooms, which had been sealed off from the rest of the world by thick layered curtains, the air looked hazy and brown. Of course, the smoky air wasn't the worst of Kartek's worries. It only made the afternoon heat even more insufferable than it already was.

Rounding the final corner to the meeting room, she thanked the Maker for the thousandth time that day that Hedjet's customs of dress were not like those of their northern neighbors. Kartek had never understood the need for a woman to wear so many layers of clothing, nor for those layers to be so long. Whenever the fine northern ladies ventured to the southern realm for politicking of some sort, they always looked miserable. Queen Louise of Destin had even fainted once.

Kartek paused briefly on the white arched bridge between the main palace and its meeting tower to glance down again at the sea of caravans and tents sitting just outside the city. So great were their numbers that they stretched from the edge of the city walls all the way out to the edge of the city's crops that lined the foot of the northern mountains. Kartek's heart faltered a little as she imagined so many unfriendly bodies so close to her people.

Not only had the tribes come to wait outside the city walls, but hundreds of tents now covered the sand, and they showed no sign of leaving anytime soon. Women and children flocked to the smaller outer wells and pools that lined the outside of the city walls. Men met in groups, though none crossed the invisible boundaries that separated each tribe. Camels, donkeys, and sheep also crowded around the outer pools, despite the troughs that were already filled with perfectly good water a little further out. Kartek wanted to gag as she thought of what the water in the pools might look like when the animals were done with them.

Where was Gahiji?

"Their ability to move nearly undetected in such large numbers is a bit disturbing, don't you think?"

Kartek jumped at the voice but only shook her head as Ahmos came to stand beside her. His shaven head and chest shone with sweat even though they stood in the shade of the bridge's overhang. His pleated kilt stuck to his legs, making the usually pristine alder look uncharacteristically rumpled. Even the Alder's Medallion he wore around his neck looked steamy.

"I still don't understand. The tribes never come to us if they can help it. That's why they have a Rayis. Why build camp outside the city together? And why all ten tribes at once?"

Ahmos's frown grew more pronounced. "I get the feeling we will know as soon as we enter that room." He took her by the shoulders and turned her so they were standing face-to-face. "Before we go in there, I need to remind you that while the tribes are technically our allies, they are brutal peoples. They generally think little of spilling one another's blood and will think even less of spilling ours. Whatever has them united—"

"United?" Kartek snorted, nodding down at the people below. "Even from here one can see that they would rather slit one another's throats than stand side-by-side as tent neighbors."

"The fact that they haven't yet begun to slit throats," Ahmos finished patiently, "means they're united in a single cause. And that can only mean they will be more agitated now than ever before."

Kartek nodded as she chewed the inside of her lip. "Why do you think Gahiji didn't come instead? He's the Rayis. He should be the one here, not all of them."

"That is what has me worried." He paused and glanced up and down her person before tugging on one of her short sleeves, straightening her ridiculously heavy golden headdress, and gently prying her hand off the jewel that hung from her neck. Kartek knew he must, but she immediately missed the gentle thrumming the smooth stone created between her fingers.

"Try not to look so nervous. They will be able to sense your anxiety. We must tread the line between demanding respect and imposing our authority. They might be many, but this is our land, and you are jahira here. They are only here still because you chose not to have the warriors chase them off." His dark eyes searched hers with an unnerving intensity. "You might be young, but you are jahira," he repeated. "Do not forget that."

Out of the corner of her eye, Kartek saw a movement from behind one of the great sandstone pillars. Though she knew Ebo would say nothing at the meeting, her faithful eunuch's presence would at least remind her to stay strong. As would Ahmos. She nodded.

"I understand."

She straightened her shoulders and lifted her chin as she

finished crossing the bridge. *You were born with the beauty of a queen and the sharp corners of a king,* her mother had used to say. *No wise man would dare cross you.*

If only she could believe those words now. Her jaw was set firmly, but inside, her bones felt like they had melted into a puddle.

Somehow, the meeting room with all its curtained windows and dark rugs looked even more stifling than the blinding, parched afternoon outside. Kartek walked in but waited at the entrance until all ten of the tribesmen and women had stood. Some stood more readily than others, but eventually, she was confident enough in their respect for her title, if nothing else, to take her seat before the semicircle of cushions that her servants had laid out on the rug. She could sense Ebo taking his place to her left as Ahmos sat to her right, and their presences made her feel slightly better.

But only slightly.

Once again, she looked at each of the ten faces until she had made eye contact with every single one, just as her father had taught her. Then she nodded at Ahmos, who stood.

"The jahira wishes for you to know that her intent is honest and her desire for peace is great. Understandably, however," he said, his voice growing sterner, "she is curious as to the nature of your unexpected coinciding arrival. She also wishes to know why your Rayis was not sent instead. Hopefully he is in good health."

At first no one spoke. A few glanced at each other warily while others remained impassive.

"I find it rather disturbing that you would deny us such information," Ahmos said, enunciating each word with a cool, punched emphasis, "considering that we have already shared our water sources with you since you arrived unexpected at our gates."

"I fear we bear ill news about your betrothed," one of the more luxuriously dressed women finally spoke up. Though Kartek couldn't recall exactly which tribe she belonged to, her nearly night black skin gave her away as belonging to one of the southernmost tribes.

"What about Rayis Gahiji?" Kartek spoke for the first time, hoping her voice wouldn't betray her apprehension.

"Jibril?" The woman glared across the semicircle. "You should be the one speaking. The Rayis was of the Ibhari."

Was one of his tribe?

"An enchantress attacked us." The man named Jibril stared at the ground, his arms crossed over his chest.

"All of you?" Kartek asked.

"She began with our tribe. Then she moved on to the others. We fled here because she drove us toward you."

"And the Rayis?" Kartek wanted to leap out of her seat and shake the man until he answered her.

"Rayis Gahiji is dead."

Kartek sucked a breath in. And when she looked over at Ahmos, he looked just as shocked as she was.

But that was wrong. Ahmos always knew what to do.

"And . . . and the Rayis's family?" Ahmos asked.

"His brother is dead. So are most of our warriors."

"Wait," one of the older men put up a hand. "What about—"

"They are all dead!" The small room echoed with the force of Jibril's words.

Taking a deep breath, Kartek leaned back and nodded for Ahmos to continue. She should be the one questioning them, but she knew such was impossible. Seeming to sense her distress, he began to press for details. Kartek couldn't focus on even his words, however.

Gahiji was dead.

She tried to take stock of how she felt. After years of engagement, visiting back and forth and touting the benefits of an alliance between the jahira of Hedget and the leader of the ten tribes of the Megal Desert, he was gone. There one minute, raging and roaring with the strength and vivacity of a lion, and gone the next.

If she was being honest with herself, she really couldn't put a name to the emotions racing about inside her. Anxiety for her people? Sorrow that so many of the tribespeople had been killed in one blow? Angst over antagonizing any of the tribes? Most definitely. But sadness for the loss of her betrothed? She really couldn't say.

Did that make her a bad person?

". . . know anything about this enchantress?" Ahmos was asking. "Who she is or what she wants?"

One of the older men shook his head, his turban falling slightly to the side to reveal his silver hair. "She only appears and disappears. After attacking the Rayis and his warriors, she began to go after the rest of us." He gestured at the window. "It is why we are here. She has chased us from our lands and we had nowhere else to find water or food." He turned a critical eye on Kartek. "Our remaining warriors are out fighting her now. You can see the smoke from their efforts."

So that was where the smoke was coming from. She shivered as she realized just how close the battle really was. It had to be less than a day's ride from the palace. Less than a day's ride between a rampaging enchantress and Kartek's city full of babies and children and elderly and innocent tradesmen, innkeepers, herdsmen, and farmers that had never lifted a weapon a day in their lives. She pressed her clammy hands into her dress and willed them not to visibly tremble.

The old man continued. "With our new status as allies, we

believed you would be hospitable enough to provide us with ample food and shelter until we had ousted the enemy." He held her gaze as though daring her to challenge the assumption. "And, of course, the fruits of your power, Jahira, for our injured men."

Kartek leaned toward Ahmos. "Has our treaty been ratified yet?" she whispered.

"No," he whispered back, "not until you are married to their Rayis will it be signed."

She turned back to the ten unsmiling faces. It would be wiser to allow Ahmos to address them, but she could see in their expressions that they believed her little more than a child. It was time she set them straight. That, and she desperately needed a distraction from the thoughts running in circles around her head.

"My head alder informs me that the treaty is not valid until I am wed to your Rayis. And while I am willing to provide what supplies we can spare for your women, children, and elderly, what guarantee do I have that you and your peoples will obey our laws? We are a kingdom of peace." She eyed the older tribesman back. "We will not tolerate petty fights or honor killings. It is not our way."

One of the younger men stood up so fast he nearly stumbled. "You cannot dictate to us how we shall deal with our own people—"

"You are on my land now," Kartek said, making sure her voice sounded as icy as the summer day outside was sweltering. "If you wish to intrude on our hospitality, particularly as you came uninvited, you will follow our laws." She glared at him.

"Jahira."

Kartek turned to the woman who had spoken. This woman was older than the first, dressed in a thin scarlet shirt with matching loose, light trousers, and her gray hair flowed freely all around her, covering her shoulders and back. Despite her fierce appearance, she looked more reserved and far more like a mediator than the last man, who was still glowering at Kartek from the side.

"I do not know how familiar you are with our customs, but we are all our own peoples and cannot control one another. It is part of the reason we are nomadic. If no one owns much land, it is more difficult to find a reason to kill one another. For even we fight amongst ourselves often."

Kartek listened in somewhat sickened awe. The woman spoke so calmly of feuds and death. As though such behavior was only to be expected.

"Only the Rayis, a man with the blood of all ten tribes, like Gahiji," the woman continued, "has the power of the Warrior's Song--"

"The Warrior's Song?" Kartek leaned forward. "What is the Warrior's Song?"

A few of the other tribal leaders sent the woman glares, and a few even hissed, but the woman continued, unperturbed.

"The Warrior's Song can only be sung by the Rayis and his descendants. Granted, a few that land lower in the bloodline may be able to use it on a group here or there, but only the true Rayis's song is strong enough to command us all."

Kartek frowned. "So Gahiji had the power to command all of the tribes? And he never did?"

"It is not a simple thing to use the song," the woman said. "It takes great effort and strength, and will suck even the great Rayis dry if he is not careful to use his gifts wisely."

"What does it sound like?"

"I cannot describe it. Each Rayis sings it differently. All you and your people need to know is that we currently do not have one." She drew in a long breath. "I cannot speak for the other tribes. But as for my people, we shall strive to abide by your laws."

The woman cast a dangerous glance at everyone else. "I suggest you all consider doing the same until a new Rayis can be found."

"You *do* know where the next Rayis will be found, don't you?" Kartek said. Surely they kept track of bloodlines for these sorts of situations. All the while, she prayed, *Please, Maker, don't let it be a child.* Losing Gahiji was bad enough. Her parents had spent years choosing the perfect husband. Waiting ten more years to marry while a boy child matured was the last thing Kartek wanted to contemplate now.

Nine heads turned to look at Jibril once again.

"The Rayis's line runs in your tribe," someone snickered. "Surely you know who will be next."

But Jibril just studied his hands, brow furrowed.

"Well?" Ahmos prompted. "Do you or do you not have another in your tribe who could be Rayis?"

"I've heard rumors—" the older tribeswoman began, but Jibril cut her off.

"I will need to study the bloodlines again!"

Kartek shared a glance with Ahmos.

"We were under the assumption, of course," the man with the temper said, "that you would send your warriors to join ours."

Ahmos bristled. "And why would you assume that?"

"The enchantress is now on your side of the river." He crossed his arms and looked down the bridge of his nose at Ahmos with a mean smile. "Which means she is no longer in our lands, but in yours."

As much as Kartek wanted to wipe the smirk off his face, she could only stare. This enchantress might have attacked the tribes first, but now she was in Hedjet's territory. The order of invasion couldn't have been accidental. The tribes first, now Hedjet. This enchantress was playing a dangerous game.

And winning, it seemed.

"It appears we are now involved in a war whether we wish to be or not," Ahmos said to her quietly.

Kartek held his gaze for a long moment before giving him one slow nod. Bracing herself for their wrath, she addressed the group. "My head alder and I will meet with the other alders and our commander. We will consider how to proceed from here."

"But the battle is—" the younger woman began to protest.

"In the meantime," Ahmos snapped, "we will have food delivered to your camps, as much as our stores can spare. And in return, the jahira and the alders expect that more work will be done to find the next Rayis." He turned and glowered at Jibril, who glared back for a long moment before breaking it off with a curt nod.

Kartek stood and everyone else followed suit. She only allowed herself to breathe, however, after she had left the stifling room. Once they were far enough ahead of everyone else on the bridge, she dared to mutter, "The alders won't like this."

"Commander Fadil won't either." Ahmos kept his stride smooth and his expression relaxed, but the crinkles in his face looked even deeper than usual. For the first time in her life, Kartek thought Ahmos's appearance finally matched his years. Since he kept no hair to gray, and his arms were as strong as ever, it was easy to forget that he was old enough to have been her father's best friend. But now his shoulders drooped just enough to make him look beaten. Not that she blamed him. She was weary, too.

"How are you?" He turned to her, his eyes unusually gentle.

She shrugged and went to stand by a window that faced the fields, now separated from the palace by the numberless tents squeezed tightly into their respective camps. "I do not know. I know I should be mourning the loss of my betrothed, but I fear I'm mourning the wrong loss."

"Oh?"

Kartek squeezed her jewel, taking comfort in its familiar warmth as its heat swirled about in her hand. "I am saddened by Gahiji's death, of course, but . . . I fear I am even more sorry that I have lost the betrothal itself."

"I don't understand."

Kartek turned to him. "My betrothal to Gahiji was the last thing my parents gave me before their deaths. That they had chosen a man for me before they died was a gift in itself. I knew the kingdom would have a good emeeri, and that through the marriage, our alliance with the ten tribes would benefit the entire region. But this enchantress . . . whoever she is, has rendered vain all those wise decisions and dreams in a single swoop." She took a shaky breath. "I have no war experience, and not even an emeeri on the horizon to help me rule."

Kartek felt a hand on her shoulder, and she willed herself not to shed the tears that wanted so much to come. Instead, she closed her eyes and pretended it was her father's hand there to comfort her instead.

"I wish I could offer comfort," he said quietly. "All I can say is that the Maker has a hand in this somehow. We will simply have to wait and see what happens." He sighed. "I will speak with Jibril again. That man is hiding something, and I want to know what it is." He looked back at her. "But in the meantime, try to have peace. Things will work out. They always do."

CHAPTER 3

TEN MINUTES

Here are the bandages, Jahira.”

Kartek wiped a bead of sweat away with her forearm before turning to the woman and giving her a tired smile. “Thank you, Nuri.”

“Jahira, you are tired. You should rest.” Nuri nodded at the cart Kartek was standing in front of. “My girls can pound those powders just as well as you. You will have more than enough work once the warriors return.” She looked around the tent at the countless cots and carts of healing supplies similar to hers. “Really, we have done about as much as we can. All these cots need now are warriors to fill them.”

Kartek considered arguing with the healer. She had sent Commander Fadil and several hundred of his men out to the river to join the tribesmen just the night before, but with every moment, dread seemed to hang heavier over her head like a noose waiting to tighten, and sleep had refused to come. Had she done the right thing?

A number of the alders had vehemently disagreed with the idea of sending the soldiers. Bennu, in particular, had made her dissent perfectly clear. And though Kartek had very little affection for the ill-humored old woman, she'd secretly shared many of the fears Bennu had very loudly voiced before all of the alders the day before.

How did they know if the tribesman were still even fighting? They might have been slaughtered by now, and sending Hedjet's soldiers after the warriors would be sending them to their doom. Even riding their fastest, her men wouldn't have reached the battle site until early this morning, especially as they had brought a number of caravans with them full of weapons and supplies. Or what if, Bennu had argued, the tribes were merely trying to lure Hedjet into a massive trap, emptying the city of its commander and best fighters before turning and overrunning the walls? Besides, even if they were telling the truth, Kartek was doing more than her fair share by sharing water and food with the tribes. She and her people really needn't do more.

At one point in the meeting, Kartek had wondered if they would ever reach a consensus, so it had surprised and relieved her when Commander Fadil himself had stood.

"The tribes do not live in harmony as it is, and they have been nomadic now for over a thousand years. They rely on their Rayis to keep the peace and deal with other kingdoms, such as ourselves. No, I believe they are telling the truth, or they would have slaughtered one another by now in such close quarters. Furthermore," he had fixed Bennu with a heavy glare, at which she had scoffed and looked at the ceiling, "I have had reports from scouts at our southern villages that a great number of warriors have been spotted by the river, as well as," he paused and looked around the room, meeting the eyes of all eight alders, "creatures."

So it had been decided that Commander Fadil would indeed go as soon as the sun had set. And to Kartek's disappointment when the sun had risen the next morning, smoke was still rising from the river.

"I had hoped the battle would be over by now," she told Nuri straining her eyes against the brightness of the sun as she looked southward again at the continuous column of brown and yellow smoke that still rose above the city wall. Even in the shade of the healing pavilions, to stare long at the column was nearly blinding. "Aren't most battles over in minutes or hours at most?"

Nuri let her gray hair down from its rag and retied it so her hair was off her neck. "It depends on the battle. But I will admit that I have never seen one last this long before." She pursed her lips. "All the more reason for you to get some rest. The warriors will most likely send news any time now. And I suspect we will need your skills more than ever when they do return. For that, you must be fresh."

Kartek nodded and cast one more glance around the healing tent. "How many cots do we have ready?"

"Jahira!" A small boy ran in so fast he nearly collided with Nuri.

"Is that how you address the jahira?" Nuri frowned down at the boy.

"It is alright." Kartek forced a tired smile as she bent down to address him. "What is it Ishaq? Does your father send word?"

"The men are returning!" He panted, a trickle of sweat running down his face. "My father asks that you prepare more tents for the men for healing."

Kartek lost her smile. "More? How many does he need?"

"All of them."

Kartek stared at him as she did the math in her head. How could her commander already need cots for one hundred and twenty-eight men? "You . . . you mean he needs all four tents for the injured?" She looked at Nuri in panic. "We have only prepared one!"

"He also says to tell you," the boy continued, "that there are many tribesmen who are injured as well."

Nuri's face was tight, but she looked far less panicked than Kartek felt. "Very well, Ishaq," the older woman said. "When will your father be here?"

"The scout said they will arrive in less than an hour."

Kartek knew she should say something to calm the boy as well as all of the young women around her who were now staring at them with frightened eyes, but she couldn't get her mouth to move.

"Ishaq," Nuri said, "go tell your father we will be ready. Then send your brother back to help."

The boy nodded at Nuri's words and turned to go, but not before he glanced back pointedly at Kartek. "Do not worry, my jahira," he said kindly, his dark brown eyes wide and trusting as he gazed up at her. "The Maker will spare us with your jewel and your power. You will heal all the men. I know it."

Kartek could only manage a weak smile in return. "Go," she told him.

When he was gone, she walked to the nearest cot and sat heavily upon it. "What shall we do, Nuri? I don't—"

"The enchantress is not here at the palace, Jahira. We don't even know if she's won the battle or not. Perhaps the men were able to defeat her. Besides," Nuri added in a lower voice, "you must take care with speaking so freely."

Kartek glanced up at the many faces who had paused in the plaza and on the palace steps to watch them. Though they couldn't hear her, as her soldiers were keeping the people at a distance while the cots were being prepared, she knew they were watching, judging every move she made. Many of those watching were from the tribes, coming into the market to buy supplies. They would report whatever they saw back to their tribal heads. If she wasn't strong enough, they might think it an invitation to do as they pleased. If she was too harsh, she might cut off opportunities for future peace.

No matter what she did, there was always something lacking. As if she had any more to give. Kartek leaned forward and nodded, rubbing her eyes as though doing so could remove their dark circles. "I wish Mother and Father were here."

To her surprise, Nuri sighed quietly. "I do as well, Jahira. But they are with the Maker now, and you must face this alone. It is your gift and burden."

Kartek suppressed the urge to crawl beneath the cot and refuse to come out. She couldn't hear the lecture of a jahira's burden. Not now. Not when it was weighing on her like a dune of sand. So she stood taller instead and smoothed the pleats on her dress.

"Yes. Yes, you're right. Now let's see. We will take down this pavilion tent and move all four outside the walls. Then we can treat our men and the tribesmen outside of the city." She nodded, more to herself than Nuri. "And I believe I will take your advice. I am going to refresh myself before the warriors arrive."

Nuri bowed before rattling off a list of names of the girls under her tutelage. Not that they would be of great assistance when the warriors actually arrived, but at least they could prepare Kartek's powders and bandages as more manservants set up the rest of the tents and cots.

Kartek left the shade of the expansive tent. The sun only made her sweat more, but at least there was a small breeze blowing, hot as it was. She walked back through the city's open gates toward the palace, for once, not bothering to return the greetings her people showered upon her as she went. She briefly considered going to her rooms to get away from the crowds, but Oni would only fuss over her there. Taking solace in the kitchens would mean her cook would try to stuff her full of food she had no appetite for. Visiting any of the flower, music, art, or walking gardens would mean a string of well-intentioned servants asking her how they could be of assistance at every turn.

Outside. She needed to go outside. And alone, which meant she would have to get rid of Ebo first. Suddenly, Kartek knew exactly where she needed to go. She plotted her act as they stepped into the palace's open, airy entrance. On an average day, such respite would be more than enough to satisfy her. But today, despite the open, airy layout of the palace with its cool stone floors, she was suddenly suffocating.

Taking care not to walk with too much purpose, Kartek casually turned left down the innermost hall and ran her hand down the intricately carved stone trellises around which vines of little red flowers were wrapped, each trellis wall serving as an inner barrier to one of the six indoor courtyards that they passed.

"Ebo," she said, pausing at the threshold of the last courtyard. "I wish to go to the women's bath."

Her eunuch didn't move an inch, only shifted his gaze directly to her, his dark brows knitting together. *Now, Jahira?* he seemed to be saying. Though he knew better than to directly question her, she could feel the disapproval rolling off him like a heat wave.

"Yes," she answered as though he had spoken. "If I am to spend hours in a sweltering tent with dying men, I should at least like to feel as refreshed as possible when I begin." She turned to the female servant standing at the door. "I am not to be disturbed."

After the servant ran into the courtyard to ensure that no one else was already bathing, she returned, opened the door wide for Kartek, and bowed. Only after the door was closed behind her, however, did Kartek allow herself to breathe freely. Sand that had blown into the stone-laden courtyard crunched beneath her sandals and got caught between her toes as she headed toward the back of the courtyard. She passed eight shallow circular holes in the ground, all sumptuously lined with the smoothest of stones and covered by white shade structures into which were carved detailed patterns and designs. The water of the little pools beckoned to her, welcoming her like an old friends opening their arms for an embrace. Even more inviting was the privacy that would have been provided by the thin trellises surrounding each pool.

But a bath was the last thing on her mind. Instead, she was merely grateful that the city wall had been built directly into the palace. And that it had a hole. Because what Kartek needed was ten minutes. Ten minutes without looking at the healing tents and worrying about directly interacting with the tribesmen. Ten minutes without the critical eyes of the tribespeople being trained on her, or even faithful Ebo watching her every move. Ten minutes where *no one* could find her and ask her one more single infernal question.

She needed ten minutes alone.

Moving from a walk to a run, she reached the great wall to find the loose stone at its foot. It took a bit of work, but she finally managed to slide the stones to the side. Slipping through the hole, she placed another stone on the other side to cover it back up. Then she ran for the well.

As she ran, leaving her palace, the city, and its great wall behind, she realized she couldn't remember the last time she'd been truly alone. Ever since her parents' illness, she had been constantly followed and fretted over by servants, handmaidens, bodyguards, alders, and anyone else who could find a way into the palace. Ahmos was fond of reminding Kartek that her people's concern for her was nothing to scorn. She agreed with him, of course, but she couldn't help feeling sometimes . . . or often, rather, that so much love could be rather stifling. Just like the desert heat that was now beating down upon her head and back.

It took her less than two minutes to reach the abandoned well. She wasn't sure why it was abandoned, as its water was still good, and the sturdy palms that sheltered the well were healthy and heavy with dates. But the one time she had asked about the well as a child, she'd been scolded severely for venturing out of the palace walls alone.

Now Kartek carefully lifted her pleated skirt up above her knees and sat on the well's low stone wall. She lowered the old bucket as fast as she could. Once she'd pulled it back up, she cupped her hands and lifted the water to her cheeks. Unlike the water at the palace, this water was cool, cool enough to help her clear her head and clean her face. Or it usually was. Even the cool water felt dirty today, unable to cleanse her skin decently in preparation for the blood she knew would soon cake her hands, neck, and face. The blood of men. Her men.

And Gahiji's men. At least, they *had* been Gahiji's men before he'd died and left her with not one but eleven peoples hanging in the balance.

Kartek reached behind her neck and opened the clasp of the gold chain that hung there. Pulling it down, she carefully cupped it between her hands where she might see it better, and she examined the jewel in the sunlight. The thick golden disk that encircled the pink stone had been carved with all sorts of ancient symbols, though few knew what they meant anymore. No bigger than her thumbnail, the whole pendant was the same color as the berries she'd tasted once in the northern realm, so bright in the direct light that it nearly hurt to look at.

Her mother had always made the jewel look so stately when she wore it. But after the sickness had taken them, when Kartek had been crowned jahira and the jewel had officially become hers, she'd immediately felt awkward when Ahmos had put it around her neck, much like a little girl trying on her mother's clothes. And now she was playing pretend with the fate of the entire kingdom.

Kartek could heal, but she wasn't nearly as talented or powerful as her mother had been, and on that first day as jahira, she'd been sure everyone around her knew it, from the oldest alder to the youngest child in the palace. As time had gone on, however, she had learned to draw strength from the jewel. Wearing it was like having her mother near, and its subtle power imparted a constant strength.

"Couldn't you have stayed just a little longer?" she whispered.

Something behind her snapped.

Kartek jerked her head up and tried to turn to see what could have made the sound. As she did, one of the stones she was sitting on shifted, and she nearly fell backward into the well. She caught herself just before toppling headfirst inside, but as she did, the jewel slipped out of her hands. Pink and gold briefly sparkled in the sunlight before disappearing as it sank into the dark depths of the well.

Kartek stared down into the shadows in horror. Her jewel was gone.

CHAPTER 4

PROMISES AT THE POND

"N o! No. No. No. No. No!"

But it was too late. The gold chain and its perfect pink stone were gone. As if to seal her doom, she could just make out the shouts of men and the sounds of approaching caravans in the distance. Fadil and his men would be arriving back from battle soon. Most likely there would be some clinging to life with only moments left to live. Others might have an hour or two. Hundreds, possibly, would need her healing if she was to heal the tribesmen as well. And without her jewel, they were all as good as dead.

"No, Maker!" she pleaded hoarsely, staring open-mouthed into the black bottomless well. "Anything! I'll do anything you ask! Just please let me have it back!" She briefly considered jumping in after it but banished the thought before it was complete. She knew full well she wouldn't be able to get out again, even if she found the jewel. And by the time she got the proper servants out to search for the jewel, men would be dead because she had not been able to heal them. Besides, this was the desert. She was doubtful that any of her servants knew how to swim, let alone dive into a deep, deep well.

She wanted to cry, to scream. But try as she might, she could make nothing but a guttural choke.

Maybe if she dove in, she could find it and toss it up. She would die, but the jewel would be safe. The Maker would surely bestow it on another, perhaps one of her cousins, as she had no daughter of her own.

Without considering what she was doing, she leaned forward.

The people would be upset by her death, yes. Ahmos would be enraged, hurt, and heartbroken. And yet, they might not despise her memory so much if they knew she'd died to bring hope back to her people.

She leaned farther out over the ledge.

"Did you mean it?" a soft voice asked.

Kartek nearly lost her balance again at the stranger's voice. Whirling around, she found herself staring into the most unusual face of a most unusual man.

He looked quite sickly with the skinniest arms and legs she'd ever seen, crouching beside a heap of boulders nearby. The hair on his head was mere stubble, and his skin was far whiter than even that of Kartek's allies in the north, so white it was nearly translucent. His only features that didn't make her wish to recoil in disgust were his eyes. They were a most unusual shade of green. How many people had she ever met with eyes so like jade? Nearly everyone in Hedjet and its surrounding tribes and kingdoms had brown.

"Do you mean it?" he repeated in a soft voice. "That you'll do anything to get it back?"

The sounds of shouting could be heard again from south of the palace, louder this time.

"Wh . . . where did you come from?" she asked.

"I can get the necklace for you," he said, straightening from his crouch and taking a hesitant step forward. "I'm a strong swimmer, and I know I could get your jewel."

"I . . . I need it," she whispered. With every second she wasted, more soldiers could be dying.

"I will get it for you," he said, taking another step toward her. "But I need you to keep your promise."

"What promise?"

"The one you just made to the Maker . . . that you'll do anything to get it back."

A wail went up from the direction of the healing tents.

"What do you want?" She tried to recall the last sum she'd heard from the treasury. It hadn't been Hedjet's best year in commerce, but surely she could—

"Three things. I need for you to vow to allow me to sleep in your bed and to dine with you every night. And," he kept his large eyes trained on her face, "I need the promise of your kiss."

"You mean . . ." Kartek licked her dry lips and gripped the edge of the stone wall to stay upright. "You want me to *marry* you?"

"Precisely."

"*Marry you?*" She was hallucinating. She had to be hallucinating. "I . . . I don't even know you! I don't know who you are or where you came from or . . . or even your name!" She gestured at his body. "You look like a northerner but you speak our language." Her voice began to rise to near hysterics. "Why would I marry you and entrust my people to a stranger? Or myself for that matter?" The mere thought of touching his ghoulish body with its uneven patches of hair and spindly limbs made her shudder. The idea of getting close enough to produce an heir . . . No. She couldn't even imagine the horror.

The slight spark in his green eyes made her feel as though he could read her thoughts, but he continued in a steady voice.

"Because if you do not, you will not get the jewel back, you and your people will suffer, and there will be no chance at healing or peace." He didn't blink, didn't even flinch as he spelled out her people's fate.

How did he know about the predicament of her people? And how dare he assume he knew best? She had never seen him before, she was sure of that. He couldn't possibly know what her people needed. Their customs, their aspirations, all the stories of love and hope that she'd heard while healing at the well, he couldn't know those. He couldn't fathom them. Heat gathered in her cheeks as she glowered at him. But then Kartek looked back down into the blackness of the well.

Still . . . without the jewel, she could not save her soldiers. She could help a few people, perhaps, but not hundreds. Not the thousands that would need it, should the enchantress attack a town or city. Kartek's warriors were strong, but they were spread out between smaller villages, the palace, and the capital city. And should the enchantress slaughter her warriors, her people would be defenseless. The entire war might be lost in less than a week. For who knew just what this enchantress could do? After all, she had decimated Gahiji and his men. Gahiji, who had been the fiercest warrior known to the Megal Desert.

And even if Kartek attempted to get the jewel on her own, she would most certainly drown before she ever laid a finger on it in the inky depths of the water.

Another wail went up from the tents to the north, and Kartek nearly shrieked for a guard. Surely Ebo wouldn't be so far off he wouldn't hear her. Someone would be sure to hear her. Then they would come jump into the well and fetch her jewel. But once again, Kartek remembered that not one of her people knew how to swim.

"Get it for me." She swallowed the bile in the back of her throat. "And I will marry you."

"And how will I know you will keep your word?"

She yanked a ring off her finger and shoved it at him. "This is my signet ring. It hasn't left my hand since the day my parents died because the alders placed a covenant on it to bind it to me. No force or coercion can remove it but mine."

He took the ring hesitantly. "So if I get your jewel and—"

"And I deny our agreement, then you can give this to my alders and they will know you speak the truth."

"And if I fail?"

She took a deep breath. "I suppose it will sink with you." She would never hear the end of Ahmos's lectures, but that would be the least of her worries should she lose the jewel.

He nodded and gazed down into the well. "Fair enough." Then he was gone. A splash echoed up to her from the well's depths, and Kartek closed her eyes and pleaded with the Maker to let him find it. And to also somehow save her from her awful promise.

She needed a miracle.

The sun remained at the same angle overhead, so she knew it was impossible for much time to have passed while he remained submerged. But it felt like hours. How long could he hold his breath? Could he really swim? *Let him live,* she prayed. *Let him find the jewel and live.*

Perhaps she was losing her mind, asking the Maker that he live so that she might be wed to an ugly little stranger who had extorted herself and her kingdom. But really, it couldn't be so bad to resent the idea of one more death on her hands. For by now she could hear that the caravans had returned, and the songs of mourning had already begun, echoing throughout the desert valley. She should have been there to greet them and immediately set to healing the sickest and the most injured. But instead she was here, agreeing to hand over her kingdom to a complete stranger because she had selfishly sought solitude when her people needed her the most.

Some Jahira she had turned out to be.

A splash sounded from below.

"Do you have it?" she called down.

"Not yet. But I think I know where it fell."

Kartek gripped the walls until her fingernails ached from scraping against the stones. The air rushed from her chest, leaving her empty and brittle. What had she just done? Her servants. Her people. Her soldiers. Her animals. The other kingdoms and tribes that depended on her oasis. Her future children.

Her own self.

She had just traded them all for a rock.

A gasp echoed up from the well. She leaned over its edge to peer down, just able to make out the shadow of a man emerging from the water. To her great angst, climbing the walls took him even longer than searching the water had. The stones were old and much of the mortar was soft and crumbling, but with each step he climbed he had to stop and carve out yet another grip for his hands.

More important than anything, however, was the glimmer of her jewel hanging from his neck.

Kartek was shaking so hard her knees could barely support her by the time he reached the top. But instead of handing the jewel over immediately, the stranger rolled over the well's wall and collapsed on the ground, panting so hard she thought he might pass out, his skinny limbs sprawled in odd directions as he gasped for air.

"I promise . . . Princess," he gasped between breaths. "Our marriage can save your people."

Kartek frowned. Not only had he called her *princess*, which hadn't been her title in over a year, but the manner in which he addressed her was familiar, far less formal than even that which the alders used. Who did this man think he was?

But she didn't have time to ponder details. For as soon as he slipped the thin gold chain from his neck, she snatched it up and placed it around her own, inhaling deeply as the power surged from the jewel into her heart and all the way out to her fingertips once more.

She could heal them now.

"I suppose we will—" he began, but she didn't hear the rest of his words. She was running as fast as she could toward the tents.

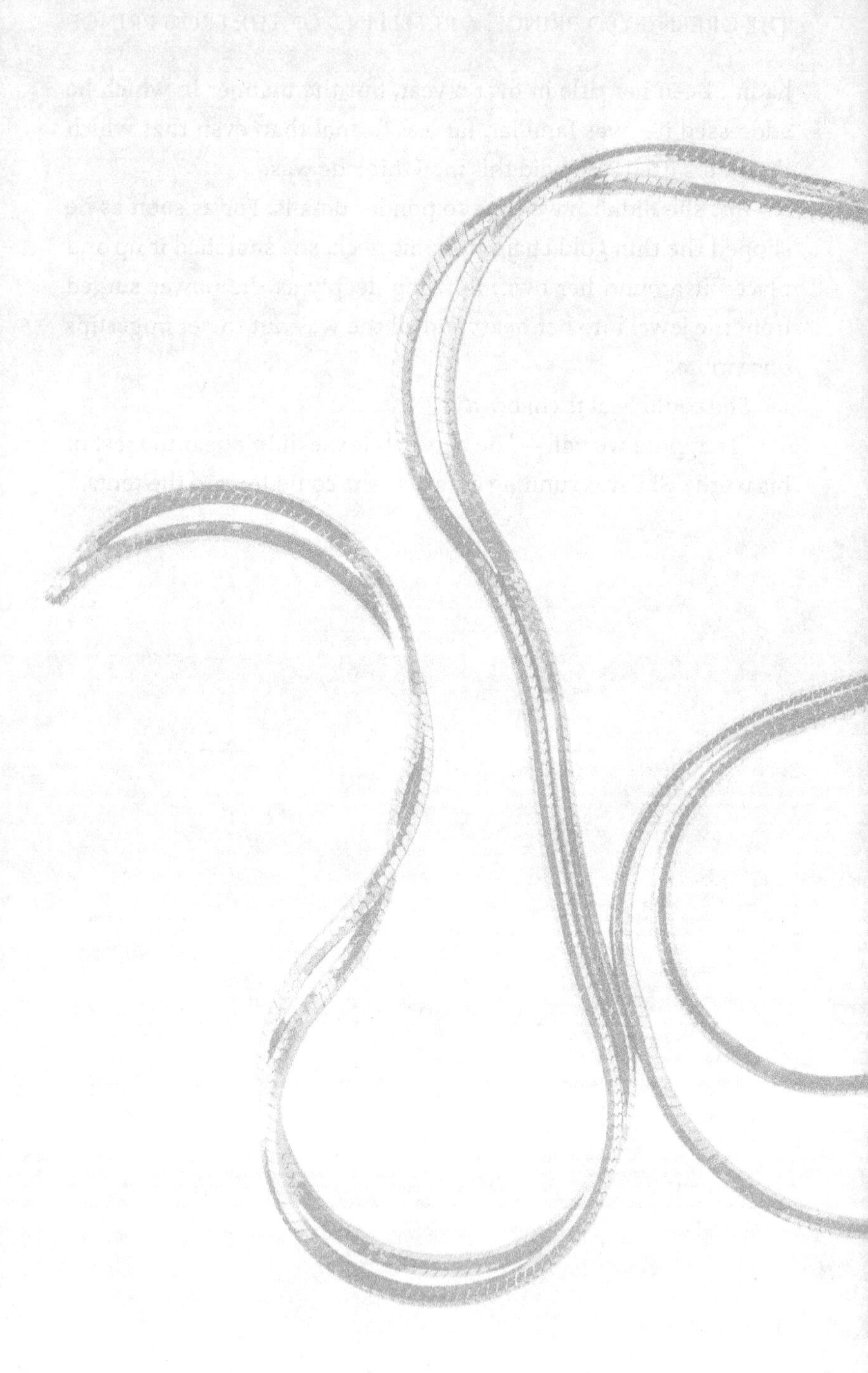

CHAPTER 5

PROMISES BECKON

Kartek ran until her lungs ached with each breath. Blindly, she shoved her way past carts, people, and even a few animals, trying to cut through the plaza to reach the main city gates. Unfortunately, however, it was the hour of evening after which the sun had sunk, and people emerged from their homes to sell, buy, and trade in the cool of dusk. No matter how fast or hard she pushed, her progress through the crowded square was agonizingly slow.

As she elbowed her way through the throng, causing cries of surprise and indignation as she did, anger began to fill the void where angst had been moments before. Anger at herself for her reckless, blind, myopic stupidity. Anger at the impudent, assuming, reptilian-looking stranger that would take advantage of her and her people in their time of need. Anger at the enchantress who would attack in the heat of the summer day and force her men to fight until they were felled not only by the sword but also by the heat.

"Jahira!"

She slowed when she heard the familiar voice. "Commander!"

she called back. Then she saw him, waving at her from the shade of the palace's front steps.

"Jahira, we have been looking everywhere for you!" He knelt before her, but she could hear the barely suppressed reproach in his voice.

She deserved far worse. "I apologize. My jewel fell from my neck, and I needed to retrieve it. What news have you?" She began walking toward the city gates, hoping to draw him away from more questions about her disastrous escapade. To her relief, he followed.

"Many have been overcome by the heat. Some should be able to rejoin the fight tomorrow, with your help, of course, but—"

"The battle isn't over?"

Commander Fadil grimaced. His dark beard glistened with sweat, and as she walked beside him, she could smell the all-too-familiar scent of death.

She hated that smell.

"I cannot tell for sure. One moment we were fighting just as we had been for an hour. The next, she was gone, along with all of her minions. Just vanished into thin air." As they moved through the city gate, he frowned at the spread of cots beneath the healing tents. Children ran free, getting underfoot despite the healers' protests and *shooing*, and animals roamed around the tents' edges even thicker than the children, probably drawn by the scents of the poultices and herbs the healers were using, as the soldiers tried to chase them off,

"I am not sure how the tribesmen managed to fight for so long without us," he said, shaking his head. "Her army is quite small, but the heat does not seem to bother them, and they are fierce." His thick dark brows knit together tightly. "I could not say for sure, but she seems to have at least a dozen under her command."

Only a dozen? What army only had a dozen soldiers? "Does

she attack our warriors herself?" Kartek asked as they neared the first tent. The smell of body odor and blood mingled even stronger in the hot air.

"Not while she controls her own forces, no. She doesn't seem to be that powerful. But her warriors are enough to deal with on their own." He stopped several yards from the edge of the tents.

In the short time since she'd been gone, three more tents had been spread out so that all four together created one gigantic covered pavilion that sat between the city's outer wall and the thousands of tribespeople. Every single cot was either filled or waiting to be filled by one of the many bodies still being unloaded from the caravans. Groaning polluted the air. Women and men, far more than just Nuri and her girls, rushed about between the cots with jars and dippers full of water, but the water seemed to do little for those who cradled wounds.

Kartek frowned. "What kind of enemy were you fighting?"

The commander looked down at her, his eyes wide and his jaw tight. "I'm afraid you will find their injuries are far from normal."

Heart pounding, Kartek tried to steel herself as she walked to the nearest man, whose cot was already saturated with blood. She held her jewel tightly in one hand as she took a deep breath and forced a smile. "Let me see," she said in her softest voice.

Instead of allowing her to peel the cloth away from his arm, however, the man let out a shriek. The commander grabbed her by the arms and yanked her back just out of the man's reach as he swiped at her, fingers raking the air where her face had been a second before.

Kartek screamed. Commander Fadil pushed her behind him as two other soldiers grabbed the man and pressed him back into the cot. He thrashed and growled at them as they pinned him down.

The commander turned back to her. "Can you heal him?"

Kartek's heart was pounding so hard she could hardly hear him. The man who had lain in the cot like a sick child just moments before now seemed to have more in common with a rabid dog than his comrades who struggled to keep him on the cot.

"Jahira?"

"What? Oh. Oh, yes. I will try." She stepped closer, though it wasn't without trepidation. With shaking hands, she clutched her jewel in one hand and reached out to him with the other. When her hand neared the bloodied bandages on his arm, he thrust his head toward it, snapping with his teeth. She jumped, but didn't step back this time. As soon as the commander had control of the shrieking man's head, she carefully forced herself to peel back the bandage.

Teeth marks, each as long as her thumb, formed a crescent moon on his arm. From one side to the other, the bite mark was as wide as a cantaloupe. She gasped and had to grit her teeth as she reached out to him once more. This time, she made contact with his flesh. In her head, she recounted the words of her mother, as she always did during a healing.

Breathe out. Her mother's voice came back to her as clearly as the stars on a summer night. *Focus on the jewel. One day you won't need to touch it as you heal, but for now, let it guide you. Remember that the Maker is the one healing. You are only the vessel. Don't fight it. Don't force it. Simply let it come.*

She felt the tightness in her shoulders begin to unwind as the familiar sensation moved within her. It was smooth, like honey rolling from her heart through her veins and down her fingertips. As she held her hand against the bite she squeezed her eyes shut, but the longer she touched him, the less the man fought.

Only after she felt the last tooth mark close did she open her eyes.

The man had fallen back onto the cot. His face was pale and shone with sweat, and she might have thought him dead except for the life she had just sensed within him. She looked up at Commander Fadil, but his face wasn't as relieved as she thought it would be. Instead, he was tugging on his black beard and staring at the other cots beyond them.

Scenes like the one she'd just quelled had erupted all over the place. Villagers screamed and ran. Some tried to escape. Others wept as they strained to keep their own warriors from harming themselves or anyone else.

"Have they done this the whole way back?" she whispered.

The commander shook his head. "That was the first."

"Well," Kartek did her best to shake her fear and straighten her shoulders. "We had better get to work."

The rest of the afternoon and far into the night was spent healing. The outbursts continued to grow in number. First it was just from the tribesmen, but then her men began to show it as well. She could only surmise that the timing of the bites had something to do with it. And to make matters worse, a number of the tribesmen, even those who hadn't been bitten, made it very clear that they wanted nothing to do with her. She wanted very much to tell them the feeling was mutual.

At first, the outbursts of the men bitten by the enchantress's creatures made Kartek cringe and draw back each time, but eventually she was too tired to react to each little hiss or lunge. The glares and muttered insults weren't so frightening either, at least not with Ebo and Commander Fadil at her side.

Strangely enough, she began to find a rhythm in the motions of healing that helped her focus. The constant demand for her attention kept her from dwelling on the awful decision she would have to make when she eventually returned to the palace. Threats uttered by angry strangers were preferable to whatever the green-eyed stranger might want after the wedding vows were said. By the time dark had fallen and lamps were lit around the tent, Kartek was too exhausted to even ponder the strange, alarming meanings of his cryptic requirements of sharing her bed and meals and a kiss.

But at last the loudest cries and groans and grunts and shouts died down. Many who had collapsed from the heat were recovering, and those who had been bitten were back in their right minds and resting, weak but safe.

"Jahira," Nuri put her hand on Kartek's shoulder, "you have done much. Leave them to me and my girls now. You will be no good to them tomorrow if you have no sleep."

Kartek leaned against a tent pole and closed her eyes. Keeping them closed was more than tempting. Her muscles ached and her clothes were drenched with sweat and blood. Staying upright was getting more difficult with each cot she visited, and she wanted nothing more than to let Oni draw her a bath in her chambers so she could bathe then curl up on her sleeping mat.

Until she recalled that tonight her mat wouldn't belong solely to her anymore.

Perhaps it would be better to remain in the tents and work until she passed out here on the dirt. Her servants would care for her, and she would be considered unfit to make any sweeping decisions for a few more days at least while she recovered. Not even a husband, or a man claiming that right, would be allowed near her while she recovered.

But that would be dishonest. She had made a promise, and even if none of her servants knew, the Maker did.

"Very well." Kartek pushed herself up and began trudging back toward the palace. She walked slowly, for her entire body ached. But each step was still too fast, for it still inevitably carried her to a fate worse than any she had ever imagined.

"Would you like me to fetch your sedan, Jahira?" Ebo finally spoke when they had made it back to the other side of the tents. The looks he sent her were accusatory, and the fact that he had dared speak at all made his wrath even clearer, but Kartek didn't bother explaining her earlier disappearance or reappearance. He would find out what had happened soon enough. They all would.

SHE HALF EXPECTED the pale skinny man to appear out of the shadows when she reached the palace steps. But she made it up the four great steps unaccosted. Even greater was her surprise when she walked through the grand archway and wide receiving hall uninterrupted as well. Only when she had sat down to a simple supper did she allow herself to breathe. Perhaps he had forgotten. Or better yet, maybe he had been a product of her imagination. She had been so worried over the men, she told herself, that it was really quite possible she had dreamt him up.

"Jahira?"

Kartek looked up from where she was slumped over her bowl of rice and dates. "Yes, Oni?"

"There is a . . . a man here to see you."

Her mouth was suddenly too dry to swallow. "What does he want?"

Oni looked around before skittering up to Kartek's side, then she glanced around once more before leaning in. "He's saying you promised to marry him. The guards tried to send him away, but he . . . he has the signet ring."

Kartek put her spoon down and closed her eyes. "Go get Ahmos."

"Should I—"

"Just go!"

The girl shuffled back before breaking into a sprint.

Kartek let her head rest on the table, ignoring the looks of concern she knew her guards and servants were sending her.

"Is this man a threat to you, Jahira?"

Kartek looked up. She couldn't remember the last time Ebo had spoken on his own accord so much in one day. Or even twice in one week, for that matter. She tried to smile, but it wouldn't come. "No, Ebo. I told him to come. But thank you." Before she could assure him more, she was interrupted by Ahmos's shout.

"Everyone out! I will counsel with the jahira alone."

Ebo glared at the alder, but Kartek sent him a pointed look at the door. Once the room was clear and all the doors and windows were shut, Ahmos turned to Kartek. In that moment, she felt the way she had as a little girl when he'd caught her stealing dates from the kitchen. His dark eyes shone in the light of the torches that were hung on each of the dining hall's eight walls, and he had fisted his hands and placed them on his hips.

"I would have had his hand and tongue cut off for such falsehoods if it weren't for the fact that Oni says he has your *ring*?"

Kartek felt the edges of her eyes prick. The bite in his voice was harsher than it had ever been.

"Well, what do you have to say?" he prodded.

She could only force her voice to a whisper. "It's true."

"What is true?"

"That I promised to marry him."

For the first time in her life, Kartek saw Ahmos fall speechless.

"I snuck out to that old well just before the caravans returned this afternoon," she said in a rush. "I only wanted a few minutes alone. I was leaning over it and I accidentally dropped my jewel into the well."

She hadn't thought it possible, but Ahmos's eyes seemed to grow even larger.

"I didn't know what to do, and then this man appeared and offered to go down into the well and get it for me."

"You didn't think to come back and send one of us?"

"He said he could swim. And I believed him. And don't tell me that anyone here knows how to swim. We live in a desert, Ahmos. This man is from the north. Or at least, I think he is. Anyway, he told me that he would get it for me if I married him." She paused, unable to look at Ahmos anymore. "I didn't think he would survive, but I had to try. The soldiers were arriving and I could hear their cries." Her voice cracked. "I didn't know what else to do."

"Well, it appears he did hold up his end of the bargain." Ahmos frowned at the round pink jewel that now lay safely against her chest. "But at what price?" He looked at the ceiling and clenched his fists. "Sandstorms and snakes, Kartek. What would your parents say? Did it ever occur to you that this man might be able to swim because he could be another one of the enchantress's tricks?"

Kartek started a little. It was the first time anyone had called her by her first name since her parents had died. Not that it mattered now. A new dread filled her belly and threatened to push out what little she had managed to eat of the rice and dates. "I don't want to marry him." A hot tear rolled down her cheek.

Ahmos's angular face softened a little and he walked over to her side and placed a hand on her arm. "What's done is done. Unfortunately, I cannot advise you to break your word now. Not when so many have seen the ring in his possession. It would undermine their trust in you and possibly bring down discipline from the Maker as well. After all, a promise is a promise." He ran his free hand over his scalp. "But we will place Ebo and a few of the others wherever you desire them."

"I'm sorry, Ahmos."

He knelt down and looked her in the eyes. "On the day of your birth, I promised your parents I would not let any harm come to you." He straightened and adjusted his kilt. Only then did Kartek see the handle of a small knife sticking out of the thin belt wrapped about his waist. "You should keep your word. But if he harms or threatens to harm you in any way, I will kill him myself."

Kartek shuddered. It was easy to forget that Ahmos had once been her father's most trusted bodyguard before he had become his favorite adviser.

He held out his hand to help her to her feet. "Perhaps I am wrong about all of this. Perhaps he will be a miracle from the Maker, sent to save us from our doom."

Kartek doubted that her newly betrothed would be anyone's savior as she recalled his bony arms and legs that seemed to stick out in every direction, but Ahmos's words bolstered her spirits enough to let her leave the dining room without crying, and the warm comfort of his arm under hers was enough to move her from the dining hall all the way to the palace's entrance once more.

CHAPTER 6

RELUCTANT BRIDE

All of her confidence fled, however, when she reached the entrance and saw him standing beneath the white archway. He looked even more unappealing and sickly than before, his skin appearing a shade greener in the torchlight than it had in the afternoon sun. The hollows of his cheeks accentuated his gauntness, and for the first time, Kartek noticed that his legs and arms all looked too long for his body. The thought of having him wrap those arms around her made her wish she hadn't had the chance to eat any supper at all.

Still, she was struck once again by the brightness of his eyes, and for a brief moment, fancied she had seen them before. But no, she had never seen anyone with a body like his. Such a repulsive man, so ill prepared to survive the brutal desert, would have been memorable indeed. She briefly tried to imagine what a future child of hers with such light skin or large green eyes might look like, but the thought made her shudder. No, she would not be bearing him children any time soon. Not if she could help it.

"Kartek." He inclined his head.

Kartek felt Ahmos stiffen beneath her arm. Such was the greeting of a peer. Not a commoner, or even an alder.

"I was glad to have your ring. It seems these men will not believe me." The stranger paused and fixed his piercing eyes on her face. "I trust you had a good reason to leave me so quickly after making our betrothal agreement."

"I needed to save the lives of my men." Kartek had to unclench her teeth to speak.

"Of course." He nodded again. "But now that the jahira has returned from her errand, perhaps we should get on with the wedding."

"What? Here? Now?" Ahmos's voice rose, but the stranger's voice stayed smooth and irritatingly calm.

"Yes. I'm afraid this is most urgent. And if I am not mistaken, is it not tradition to allow the groom's family to choose the time and date of the wedding?"

"For men of rank, yes!" Ahmos cried, dropping Kartek's arm and moving to stand between them. "But what are you to make such a demand? Who are you?"

The thin man opened his mouth as though to speak, but nothing came out. Finally, he shook his head. "You may call me Dakarai."

"Of . . ."

"Dakarai will do."

"Of course it will," Ahmos muttered before turning to the servants. "Very well. Let's get this over with. Call the holy man into the throne room. Fetch the alders and have them wait for me there as well. Tell them I will explain later." He chased the servants out, shouting orders and barking warnings at those who tarried. Finally, Kartek was left alone with Ebo and the man.

"I will marry you because I gave you my word," she said, taking a step closer. "But know now that my kindness is merely dictated by my honor. I will share my meals, my bed, and a single kiss with you, but nothing more."

"Jahira, I need you to be—"

"Know this as well." She took a step closer. "I will never forgive you for what you have done to me. To my people."

He raised his hands, then let them fall back to his sides. Looking down at the shiny white tiles laid out in intricate patterns, he shrugged. "I only wish I could explain. But I can only help if you keep your word."

Kartek glowered at him. "You think I can trust you after you tricked me?"

He blinked, as though surprised. "What trickery was there? I told you what I would do and I upheld my end of the agreement. I am only asking you to keep yours."

"And that is what I am doing. But expect nothing else. Not now, not ever." With that, she whirled around and marched up to her chambers with Ebo on her heels.

When she arrived in her rooms, they were already being filled with all sorts of flowers and oils. Her sleeping mat had been rolled out and two pillows lay at its head instead of one. The sight made her sick.

Though she knew little about what went on between a man and a woman after marriage, aside from the necessary details about child-rearing her mother had told her on her thirteenth birthday, Kartek was suddenly blatantly aware that not even her sleeping mat would be hers anymore. By definition, *she* would not be hers anymore. They would be one. And while she had no desire to own any part of him, he would have every right to her.

She scrunched her eyes shut and swallowed back a dry heave.

"My jahira," one of her handmaidens ran in and scurried over to her vanity, "I have been instructed to help you dress for—"

"No thank you. I will not be prepared for my wedding."

The young woman stared at her blankly. "But I have a change of clothes. Something not covered in—"

"Blood?" Kartek shook her head. "No, I will wear what I have on. This dress might not be so splattered with blood had he simply done the *honorable* thing and retrieved the necklace without wasting time and forcing me into wedlock in the first place." The beautiful dress she had tried on the day before would have to wait for the next jahira. Kartek wasn't about to mar its purity by donning it for such a farce of a union.

Kartek could see that the handmaiden wanted very much to argue. Her lips twitched a few times, but in the end, she simply bowed and left the room.

Oni came in as the girl left. In her hands was a large flat box that was lined with fabric. Inside the box lay all sorts of jewels and precious stones embedded in silver and gold bands, chains, and hooks. "As much as I know you wish to forgo tradition in its entirety," she said in a quiet voice, "there are some things that simply must be done."

Kartek sat stiffly on the stool before her cosmetics table and mirror. "Then let us get on with it so we can be finished with the whole dratted thing."

Oni gently removed each piece from the box, but before she could place any of the pieces on Kartek, another woman appeared in the mirror. Kartek turned to find Alder Cantara.

"This honor should have been your mother's," the older woman said in her deep voice, gently placing a thin, bony hand on one of Kartek's. "I would be honored if you would allow me to stand in her place."

Kartek miserably met the alder's gaze in the mirror, but there was no way she could object. The rite had to be done, and if Kartek's own mother couldn't give her such a gift, and no one had been officially chosen, as her wedding should have been a month away still, there was no one more fitting than the oldest female alder. So Kartek nodded, and Cantara took the jewels from Oni.

First, she placed a golden circlet headpiece on Kartek's head. Its single green jewel, shaped like a teardrop, hung down between her brows. "Green for the healing aloe that grows near the river. May there be healing in your love whenever you wound one another, just the way you heal those who wound themselves."

Kartek wanted to roll her eyes, but she didn't dare before the stately alderwoman.

Next, Cantara lifted from the box a pair of ruby earrings. "Red, for the blood your spouse vows to spill if anyone threatens you with harm."

If that wasn't pessimistic, Kartek didn't know what was.

"Blue," Cantara continued, holding up a golden bangle bracelet with little sapphires embedded in it, "for the days you lose loved ones and the tears you will shed together." After slipping the bangle on Kartek's arm, she placed a nose ring in Kartek's right nostril, its single jewel hardly bigger than a seed. "Yellow, for the golden days ahead and bliss with your lover."

Kartek wanted to give an unladylike snort and yank that one out, but she restrained herself as Cantara held up the final piece.

"Opal," she slipped the ring on Kartek's right hand, "white as northern snow, for purity and peace and the love that shall spring from it."

The second she was finished with the preparation ceremony, Kartek stood abruptly and strode over to the door, waiting silently as she tugged at the folds of her dress and ignored the yearning to yank all of the jewelry off. All six of her handmaidens moved to surround her. They would walk that way to the throne room, where each girl would peel away one at a time until Kartek was left alone.

"Jahira," Cantara said, coming to stand beside the little

procession where it waited at her door. "I know this is not the kind of marriage you envisioned for yourself. Particularly," her voice dropped, "just one day after you learned of the death of your betrothed. But perhaps this will not be as terrible as you think. The Maker can stop it at any time he wishes."

"Or perhaps he is merely punishing me for my folly." Kartek nodded at her head handmaiden. "Let us go."

Her sandals slapped the shiny stone floor as she walked through the open doors to the throne room. Even before they reached their destination, the happy sound of the pipe greeted them, but as with the jewels, there was no way to remove that form of rejoicing. It was required for the ceremony itself.

Unlike Kartek, her groom had changed clothes. He stood on the opposite side of the throne room, waiting to enter just as she was. Though she wasn't sure why, she was surprised that not even the regal kilt Ahmos must have chosen nor the traditional burgundy linen wrapped around his torso and shoulders made him look any stronger or any less pale. His eyes, looking even wider than usual, were fixed on the holy man at the center of the room. Only then did she realize that Dakarai, too, looked like he might pass out.

Maybe he would. Then the alders could take it as an omen and forbid the marriage. Kartek would be free because she had tried to hold up her end of the bargain, and then she could banish him forever.

But it was not to be. The music changed, and it was time for them to walk. One step at a time she slowly approached the center of the floor. She refused to be impressed that he knew how to walk to the rhythm of the music or that he properly knelt before the holy man and knew to put only his right hand forward at the holy man's feet. Ahmos must have taught him that.

She also knelt and placed her left hand next to his. Where the blades of their hands touched his skin was cool and clammy, and she had to ignore the ripple of fear and disgust that roiled in her stomach.

"Since the time of Hedjet's birth," the holy man began, "each jahira has married a man of righteousness and peace so that the kingdom and all its people may see prosperity and goodwill as each generation rises and falls. The jahira vows to guard the jewel and all her powers that are connected to it, and the emeeri vows to protect both of them with his life if such a call comes." He looked at Kartek. "Are you ready to recite the vows, my jahira?"

No.

"Yes, Holiness."

"And you?" He turned to Dakarai. "Oh, but I don't believe I have received your name."

Kartek couldn't stop herself from glancing up at him. If he told the truth, she could have messengers sent out to find out more about this man's history. She would send word as far as Destin if she had to. Surely King Rodrigue would come to her aid. And if he lied? Well, that would make their marriage as real as a mirage.

"Dakarai of the Ibhari tribe."

So that's how he knew of her people's customs. She could hear some of the alders release sighs of relief as her hopes went up in flames. His own people were camping at the city gates.

"Then rise, Dakarai, son of the Ibhari, and swear your allegiance and life blood to this people." The holy man held up a jewel. It was nearly identical to Kartek's, small and round, nearly the size of her thumb, surrounded by a thin gold disk. The only difference was in the color. Instead of pink, this one was onyx. "For with this jewel I give to you, the jahira's people are now your people. Their struggles are your strife. Their joys are your delight, and their safety is your design." He held up the jewel's chain with both hands. "Do you swear it on your life and before the Maker? To guard them with your last breath?"

"I do." There was no hesitation. No moment of thought paused his answer. It was as if this vow had been his goal the whole time. Kartek wanted to stop watching him, but she couldn't pull her eyes from his face. There was a strange sort of determination in his unusual green eyes. Again, she was struck with the feeling that she had seen them before.

"Then I now declare you Dakarai, emeeri of the Hedjetian people."

The curiosity that had played in the back of Kartek's mind vanished as he turned to face her, nerves and revulsion taking the place of her curiosity. Slowly, Dakarai removed the veil. Placing his hands on the sides of her face, he gently pulled her forward to place a soft kiss on the bridge of her nose and each of her eyes. She trembled as he then moved in for the last of the ceremonial kisses. His breath was warm on her lips where he briefly paused.

The kiss was not as she expected it to be. His hands might have been cold and clammy, but his lips were warm and inviting as they tenderly pressed against hers.

And she had the ridiculous inclination to kiss him back.

Before she could decide whether or not to act upon the traitorous thought, however, he pulled away and let go of her hands before bowing to the holy man.

So great was her distraction that Kartek nearly forgot to bow as well and didn't recover her senses until they were on their way to her chambers.

Their chambers.

A whole new wave of angst took her, and it was all she could do to keep her feet moving forward and her hands from trembling as two servants opened the door to the hastily created honeymoon suite.

HE STOPPED JUST inside the door and looked around the room.

The fire had been built in the brief time she'd been gone, and even more lily petals had been scattered all about the floor as well as on the sleeping mat. Countless pillows had been tossed on the mat, too, and a small plate of nuts, fruit, and sweet delicacies had been laid beside the wine.

Kartek's heart wrenched. This night shouldn't have come so soon. It should have come for someone she truly loved. Someone she wanted.

It should have been with Gahiji. She had prepared herself for such a time with him. Not this stranger. Not on a whim. Something inside of her hardened.

"You may sleep anywhere you like." Kartek picked up a few of the pillows and dropped them at the bottom of the mat. "I will sleep here."

"At the foot?" His voice was soft in its surprise. "Surely that's not a fitting place for a jahira to spend her wedding—"

"If you think I will be spending tonight with you, you are sorely mistaken."

"I did not mean in that way." He avoided her gaze. "I merely meant I would take the foot of the bed."

She shook her head and ran her hands through her hair, removing the headdress and placing it back in the box on the cosmetics table, though it was hard not to let her surprise show. She had expected him to argue, to try to convince her to do otherwise. Even in their limited courtship meetings, Gahiji had made it clear that he'd expected her to give him an heir less than a year after they were wed.

The faster you bring forth a child, the faster we will be able to protect our heritage and our peace, he had said, a confident smile on his lips.

"Of course," she had agreed wholeheartedly, though the thought had made her blush more than a little. This, of course, had made him laugh even harder.

But there was no Gahiji tonight, and as her . . . husband, Kartek shuddered at the thought, was not protesting, Kartek pushed together a pile of cushions at the bottom corner of the mat closest to the fire before marching into the next room over to change into her night dress. She half expected Dakarai to follow, but he didn't. When she reemerged, he was sitting cross-legged on his half of the bed, studying one of the date cakes.

To his credit, she didn't miss the blush that rose to his pale cheeks when she walked in, nor the way he averted his eyes nearly immediately. But she couldn't let that soften her, not when she was working so hard to stay confident and strong.

"Something to eat?" He held up the little plate of food.

Kartek nearly retorted that she was far from hungry, but then she recalled that odd part of her promise, that she allows him to eat from her plate. With a huff, she took a handful of nuts and sat. "It would be wise of you to get some sleep," she said, studying her food with too much interest. "The first hour of the morning has already passed. I will be rising at the sixth." She curled up on her half of the mat and wrapped herself in a cocoon of blankets. They offered little protection, but at least she could have the illusion of being safe while she slept.

"Very well," he said, swallowing the remains of a date cake. "But Princess?"

There was that title again. "Yes?"

"You need not fear me."

"I'm sure you can understand my lack of confidence in your words."

"Completely." He spoke as though they were merely discussing crop irrigation or some other inane topic. "But I promise, I will not touch you. Not without your permission."

Kartek didn't stir, but she feared he might hear her breath quicken beneath her covers.

"Did you hear me?"

"Thank you . . . I suppose," she said. "That is quite . . . decent of you."

"And Princess? You don't need that knife beneath your pillow, either." There was a smile in his voice this time, as though he were amused.

Kartek wanted to curse. She thought she'd hidden her little jeweled dagger well.

But when he spoke again, his voice was serious. "No harm will come to you tonight. I made a promise to protect you. And I intend to keep it."

CHAPTER 7
WHATEVER METHODS

Kartek stretched then stiffened as panic seized her. But when she looked for the man at the head of her bed, she found herself quite alone. She sat up and studied the room through bleary eyes. In fact, he wasn't in the room at all, nor, when she got out of bed, was he in any of the dressing, sitting, or receiving rooms that were adjoined to hers.

Well, if her husband was the kind that appeared at night and then disappeared again the next morning, leaving her alone as much as possible while they were together, that would suit her just fine. As she took up the morning meal that had been laid out for her, however, she couldn't ignore the bit of guilt that ate at her stomach along with the hunger. Aside from a forced marriage, his actions had been completely honorable. She'd never heard of a man content with spending his wedding night alone.

"Oni," she asked when her friend came in to collect her food, "where has my husband gone?"

Oni avoided her gaze as she lifted the tray and began to arrange the empty dishes. "I believe he is down with the children."

"The children?"

"The tribal warriors' children. The ones that were playing down by the healing tents yesterday."

That was . . . unexpected. "Thank you, Oni." She glanced at the rumpled pile of clothes by the window. "He is wearing clothes, isn't he?"

Oni smiled for the first time and blushed. "Do you think Ahmos would have let him out of the palace without them? No, Ebo was sent to deliver the new clothes early this morning. He was not happy to be given the duty of an errand boy, but . . ."

"But Ahmos didn't know what to expect. I see." She paused. "What's wrong?"

Oni shook her head, still studying the tray of dirty dishes before her. "I was just hoping you were . . . well, after last night."

"Ah. Well, I am grateful for your concern, but I will admit that he was more than honorable in at least one way."

Oni finally turned to look at her, eyes the size of dates. "So you're—"

"Thank you, Oni. That will be all for now." She stood to go to her dressing room, but paused on the threshold. "Is there any more news of the enchantress?"

At this, Oni's round face clouded. "A runner arrived this morning to tell us that she had appeared in a nearby village. When the runner left, she wasn't doing much, but she and her creatures were camped just outside the town. Commander Fadil has already left with more warriors."

"Which village?"

"Maisef."

Kartek nodded. "Thank you for telling me. Let Nuri know that I will be down shortly."

"Would you like some help getting dressed today?"

"Thank you but no. I can manage on my own."

Though she was in a hurry to check on her men, Kartek relished the short time alone. Now that her rooms were apparently no longer hers, she would not take a single moment of solitude for granted again. Being surrounded by many people quickly tired Kartek out, which made the position of jahira one that required her constant effort. She had found out at a young age that she needed several hours a day to recover from the strain if she was to do much healing. The only reason she'd been able to heal so many the day before with so little rest was because of the driving fear that had lain in her heart. Now, she thought sadly as she ran her hand lovingly over the doorframe, she would be sharing even those few precious hours with someone else.

Still, she felt more prepared for the day after giving herself a quick scrub down with the sponge and clean water in the basin Oni had left. Washing away the blood from the day before felt good, though she would most likely need another bath tonight. She donned a simple dress of green and pulled her hair up into a knot before deeming herself presentable.

On her way out to the pavilion, Kartek slowed to watch the children from afar. Sure enough, Dakarai was with them. She needed to move on and speak with the commander, but something urged her just to stay and watch for a few moments more.

"Behold!" he shouted, throwing his arms up with his hands bent like claws. "I am the troll of this cave! Who dares to enter my lair?"

The children shrieked and tripped over one another as he took an exaggerated step toward them. One brave little boy grabbed a stick and pointed it at Dakarai.

"So," Dakarai turned to the little boy and took another step, raising his arms even higher. "You wish to be eaten today, do you? I think I shall have you with my squash tonight!"

Against her will, Kartek smiled as he grabbed the little boy and lifted him in the air. The move seemed surprisingly effortless for a man with such dreadfully skinny arms. The boy squealed and shouted as Dakarai walked toward the other children, still holding the child in the air.

"Who else wants to be my supper?" he growled down at them.

The children scattered, but as they did, one of the little girls stumbled and cut her knee on a rock.

Kartek had automatically taken a few steps toward them when Dakarai put the boy down and knelt at her side.

"Let me see," he said, gently taking her knee in his hands. Kartek paused as he reached back to a nearby table where herbs and salves were being mixed for the warriors. To Kartek's surprise, he grabbed a few of the bowls and began to expertly mix their ingredients together between his fingers. "This potion is magic," he told the girl, his expression serious.

Her large eyes grew wide. "Like the jahira's power?"

"Not quite so good as that," he said, dipping a finger in the bowl and tasting the mixture before throwing another root in. "But it will do for now." He took a glop of the sticky salve he'd just mixed and began caking it over the wound. As he rubbed the salve into the cut, he looked up from the wound and briefly met Kartek's gaze.

Kartek's face heated, and she quickly made her way past him into the tents. She might be jahira, but it felt foolish to get caught snooping, even if it was only at one's husband as he pretended to be a monster. She quickly set herself to work in order to forget, checking fevers and healing smaller wounds she'd missed the day before.

"Nuri, I need the Laba—"

"Here."

She started at the sound of Dakarai's voice. He was standing just at her right elbow, and he was holding out the little bowl of crushed yellow root.

"Um . . . thank you." She took the bowl, blushing again. "Would you be able to fetch me the—"

Before she could finish, a bowl of orange powder was in her hands as well. She blinked at it a few times, accepted the bowl, then turned back to the soldier's wound. "You certainly are knowledgeable about healing medicines."

He shrugged. "I had quite a bit of spare time every night once my sisters were in bed or off with their nurses. I thought I might learn something useful while I waited for my brothers to return."

Kartek turned and stared at him. "Who are you? Really?"

He frowned. "To be honest, I'm not sure where I stand now. I know what I should be. But I also know that such a position may no longer even exist."

Could the man be any more vague if he tried?

"Could you at least tell me how old you are?"

"Twenty and one. I'm curious, though," he said, gesturing to the wound she was wrapping. "You can heal with your hands. Why go through so much trouble to dress and treat the wound as well?"

"My ancestors found long ago that we can heal the worst of wounds with the jewel, but it is wise to be safe and dress it properly anyway. It prevents infection should the wound reopen in my absence."

"Can you heal without the jewel?"

"Small cuts and bruises, yes. My mother said that one day I would learn to draw more power on my own, but that will not likely be for many more years. It requires a great deal of focus and practice, and the jewel helps me channel that focus now." She fastened the bandage and put her hand on the sleeping warrior's shoulder. "There. He should be himself in a day or so." She turned to push the cart to the next cot only to find that Dakarai had already moved it for her. Shaking her head to herself, she followed.

"What is it?" he asked as she leaned down to peer at the gash in the second man's lower calf.

"I only . . . I suppose I wasn't expecting a husband with knowledge of healing. My father preferred matters of state." She glanced at him. "I don't know how much you know of my ancestry, but only the women in my family carry the gift. That's why the line is continued through the jahira instead of the emeeri. Where did you learn so much while your sisters were . . . sleeping, was it?"

His thin face darkened, and his fingers gripped the roll of bandage until they lost what little color they had. "Suffering takes on a new light when you're—"

A shout broke the stillness of the morning. Kartek and Dakarai looked up to see one tribesman trying to strangle another.

"You stole it!" the one on top shouted. He had his hands wrapped around the other tribesman's throat. "And you will return to me what you have taken!"

The other man tried to push him off, but his arms soon began to flail helplessly, each movement weaker than the last.

By the time Dakarai reached him, with Kartek close on his heels, the second man's face was nearly blue. With a surprising strength, Dakarai yanked the first man off. Kartek ran to the side of the one on the ground as other tribesmen and warriors reached them. She could feel the tension rising in the air around them as she struggled to open his airway. Finally, it opened with a satisfying pop.

"I want to know his name and tribe!" she called over her shoulder to Dakarai. When he didn't answer, she turned back to see why.

She had expected to see him keeping the man in a strangle-hold, possibly even wrestling him to the ground. Instead of restraining the man, however, Dakarai was whispering in his ear. Kartek and the rest of the men and women around her watched in awe as the man lay back down without a fight, docile as a kitten. In a moment, his eyes closed, and he began to breathe deeply.

"There you are, Jahira. I've been looking for you."

Kartek turned to find Ahmos. At the sound of the head alder's voice, many of those gathered around them began to shuffle away, though not without a few hostile looks. Ahmos bowed then glanced around. "Did I miss something?"

Kartek looked back to see what Dakarai might say, but to her surprise, he was already gone, the man he'd just put to sleep snoring quietly on his cot.

"Did you see that?"

"See what?"

Kartek shook her head. "Dakarai just broke up a fight and saved this man's life . . . by whispering to the other one and putting him to sleep."

Ahmos glanced at the sleeping man then down at the body that Nuri's girls were preparing to carry back to his cot. "This keeps getting more and more interesting," he muttered quietly. Then he turned back to Kartek. "Do you think I might have a word with you?"

"Say what you wish, Ahmos. You always do." She stood and dusted her hands off. "Did you inquire of the Ibhari tribe about Dakarai?"

"May I have a word in *private*?"

They left the healing tents and stopped at one of the outer pools. Women and children had been washing and drawing water from the pool, but one look from Ebo sent them scattering by the time Kartek and Ahmos reached it. Kartek kept her face smooth and calm as she sat at the pool's edge on one of boulders that lined the water. But on the inside, she was dreading whatever it was that he had to say. Ahmos didn't look happy. And when Ahmos was displeased, the news was sure to be dreadful.

"I have just met with the alders."

"About Dakarai, I suppose."

Ahmos sat beside her. "They are worried."

"I can't imagine why." Sarcasm wasn't becoming of the jahira, but Kartek was beyond caring about such niceties at the moment.

"We sent warriors this morning to ask about Dakarai. And it turns out that the Ibhari tribe has no knowledge of such a man."

Hope sprang to life. If he was lying about his identity, they could have the marriage annulled. But then she recalled his sharp wit and keen sense of planning. Surely he would have schemed up a way to keep her married despite such a technicality. She wanted to wilt. Instead, she asked, "Have you spoken with Jibril again?"

His frown deepened. "Not yet. That man has a talent for disappearing."

"So the alders have turned all their efforts to Dakarai then."

"Understandably, the other alders wish to know more about him."

Kartek let out a humorless laugh. "So do I. In fact, I've spent the morning trying to learn more about him." She leaned over the water's edge and cupped her hands. Dipping them in the pool and lifting them to her face, she let the water roll down her neck and sleeves.

"And what have you learned?" he asked.

"You mean aside from the fact that he can whisper angry

tribesmen to sleep? It appears he had younger sisters and several brother. He knows a great deal of healing, and he is twenty and one years." She paused. "He seems quite good with children. Also, though he hasn't said as much, I gather that at least one older brother was his father's favorite. And that wherever he was from has seen a good deal of warfare." The memory of his glistening green eyes suddenly filled her with an unexpected sympathy for the man she was determined to despise.

"Jahira . . ." Ahmos frowned down at the water, arms behind his back even in his sitting position. "I know this was hardly the ideal union. I understand the need for it, as do most of the other alders. So hopefully that will make tonight's task less difficult, perhaps."

"Task?"

He fidgeted, looking more uncomfortable than she'd seen him in a long time. "I did not wish to ask this of you myself, but—"

"But the alders demand it," another voice called out.

Kartek looked up to see a woman with white hair and a thin, stern face approaching them. Her stomach clenched a little. "Good afternoon, Bennu." She stayed seated when the old woman bowed. She probably should have stood as well, but she was hardly in the mood to see this particular alder.

"Jahira," Bennu said with a stately nod. "I understand Ahmos was informing you of our plan for tonight's supper."

"*Your* plan?" Kartek dusted her dress off and stood to face the alder. "And I suppose I have no say in whether or not I am part of this little scheme?"

Ahmos shook his head. "Of course you have a say—"

"But the alders will be displeased if you do not," Bennu finished, her hands clasped tightly in front of her as though she were talking to a naughty child. "Your thoughtless actions have brought uncertainty upon our people, and we deserve to know who our emeeri really is."

Kartek wanted very much to remind the alder that *she*, not Bennu, was jahira, but she bit her sharp words back. Her mother wouldn't have approved of such candor. "I have already tried to talk to him," she said instead, fixing her eyes on the woman's rather garish headdress of amber so she wouldn't have to look directly into Bennu's cat-like gaze. "He was quite vague. I shall learn more over time, of course, but I do not know how you wish for me to learn his entire story in one night if he is so keen on secrecy."

Bennu's thin lips curved up into a wry smile. "You forget, Jahira. You are young and pretty enough. There are more ways than one to get a man to talk."

"Bennu!" Ahmos's voice was sharp. "That is enough! You are being disrespectful."

Kartek struggled to find her voice as the heat rose to her cheeks. "And if I do not wish to use such methods?"

"Fill the man with drink! Who cares what method you use on him as long as you learn what his purpose is? One does not simply lie in wait for the jahira to be alone and then extort her into marriage for the fun of it!"

"But remember," Ahmos said, turning to Kartek as he stepped in front of Bennu, "*you* are the jahira. It is your choice to do as you see fit." He glared back at Bennu. "Using whatever methods suit your conscience."

Kartek turned and studied the little pool. As little as she liked Bennu, she understood the fear the alders were harboring. She had felt it herself since the moment Dakarai had made his demand. What if she had doomed her kingdom by crowning a vagabond or the son of a hostile warlord? Or even worse, a servant of the enchantress herself?

And yet, there was something about him that was already making her shy away from such assumptions. Though she was still angry with him for the forced union, nothing in his conduct had been less than chivalrous since they'd said their vows. There was a gentleness about him and a near penitence in his words nearly every time he spoke that had begun to chip away at her cold, hard resentment. And though she had trusted Gahiji because her parents had chosen him for her, she had never witnessed such tenderness in her betrothed in all their years of courtship. The idea of using such underhanded methods to get Dakarai talking made her feel . . . dirty.

She turned back to Ahmos and Bennu, who were glowering at one another with impressive ferocity. "I will sup with him privately," she said. "But," she set her shoulders and turned to Bennu, "I will use *my* methods alone. And do not even consider sprinkling Mahat root in his cup. I can smell it and will have it sent to you for you to drink immediately if I find it. Are we agreed?"

For a moment, Bennu's face turned so red that Kartek thought she might collapse of heart palpitations. But the alder finally swallowed and bowed once before clutching her skirt and walking away, nose in the air.

"You treat her with too much grace," Ahmos muttered, folding his arms and looking very much like one of the angry statues in the palace courtyard. "That woman would order the birds around if she thought they would listen."

But birds weren't what Kartek was thinking about at that moment. "You were with Gahiji more than I ever was. What was your impression of my betrothed?"

Ahmos rubbed his shiny head thoughtfully. "I rarely spoke with him, only watched your parents do so. But from what I saw he was gifted at inspiring others to follow him. He could garner the support of even his most rebellious tribes." He paused. "Without using that fighting song, or whatever the tribal heads called it."

Kartek nodded. That made sense. The times she had met Gahiji before his death, once or twice a year after she had turned twelve, her betrothed had filled her with awe, making her feel uncharacteristically shy. Everything he did had purpose and was done with fervor, from the way he walked to the way he spoke. Gahiji knew what he was doing even when he didn't. Unlike her.

"Was he kind?" she asked Ahmos.

"I could not say, Jahira. I do not wish to speak wrong of the dead, and I was not present at occasions when such behavior might be witnessed."

Which was Ahmos's way of saying no.

As Kartek made her way back to the healing tents, Ebo invisible behind her as always, Kartek rubbed her head. What was wrong with her? Why was she so confused? A man had just forced her into wedlock. She dug her fingernails into the palms of her hands. She couldn't allow herself to be caught off her guard. She must remain resolved and—

"Jahira! Alder Ahmos!"

They turned back to find a young man running toward them. He couldn't have been older than fifteen years.

"What is it?" Ahmos asked as the young man stopped before them, gasping for breath.

Kartek didn't wait for his answer, however. She took him gently by the arms then pressed the palm of her hand against his upper chest. As her power moved into him, he continued to pant, but she could no longer hear his breath rattle.

"Thank you, Jahira," he whispered.

"Now what have you run all this way for?" Ahmos pressed. "From where did you come?"

"I was with the contingent at Maisef."

Kartek looked at Ahmos to find her own alarm reflected in his eyes. "Didn't Commander Fadil go to Maisef this mor—"

"Yes." Ahmos's face was hard.

Kartek turned back to the boy. "Did the enchantress attack?"

"Not yet."

"Then what happened?"

"Commander Fadil never arrived. We waited like he'd said to in his message he sent on the bird. But he never reached us, and the enchantress continues to draw closer to the village with each hour."

"Maisef is only a two-hour journey from here," Kartek said to Ahmos as she waved another servant down to escort the young man to the respite of the healing tents. "Commander Fadil had hoped she would retreat after such a fierce battle yesterday." Kartek reached up and began to rub her jewel. "First the tribes. Now us. Why us? What does she want?"

"Jahira," the young man said, pulling away from the servant that was trying to lead him to the tents. "I am afraid that is not all. The tribesmen who fought with us are in disarray, and our men cannot hold her alone. Our captain says he must have more men, or he can only delay their advance. We might be able to protect the village for a few hours, but we will not be able to stop them from coming here, should they decide to do so."

After sending him off, Kartek resumed her walk back to the palace with Ahmos, feeling more exhausted than she could remember in her life. "What do we do?"

He turned to her just outside the palace gate and rested a hand on one of its decorative iron rungs. "I swore to your parents to keep you safe. It is a vow I will die striving to uphold." Then he looked at the ground and sighed. "The alders sometimes believe they know all because you are young. While I do not agree, as I believe you quite capable of handling yourself, I do believe that their desire to know our young emeeri's truth might be more urgent than we earlier thought. Perhaps take that into consideration tonight when you're supping with your new husband."

"But what does this have to do with him? We don't know for sure that he is connected to her."

"I do not know how," he said, "but I cannot believe that his appearance during such a time of upheaval and crisis could be an accident." His eyes darkened. "And if he does happen to be a servant of the enchantress, which I pray he isn't, then there might be many, many more who will suffer the same fate as Gahiji."

CHAPTER 8

NOT SO SECRET

Kartek moved the second goblet an inch to the left before scooting it back to where it had been. Nerves warred with anger as she stared at the wine. Bennu hadn't put Mahat root in Dakarai's cup after all. She had used Ebit flower instead.

Kartek was a healer, for sand's sake. Did Bennu think her ignorant of the Ebit root? Or did she simply want to show Kartek who was really in charge?

The only reason Kartek hadn't flung the offending wine out the window just yet was because she didn't know. She didn't know how much he would tell her. *Wouldn't it be permissible? Just this one time?* she asked the Maker as she stood and went to the window to look out at the setting sun. *To protect my people? After all, he wouldn't remember after the effects had worn off . . .*

The door opened and her heart jumped as Ebo escorted her husband in.

"You look . . . refreshed," Dakarai said. His words were polite, but Kartek didn't miss the way his eyes quickly traveled down her entire person and lingered for a long second before returning to her face.

Her face flushed, though she couldn't exactly say why. He was her husband after all, and permitted to look, wasn't he? Was it really such a bad thing for her husband to think her beautiful?

"Despite whatever your impression was yesterday," she said, taking an awkward step toward him, "I do not generally enjoy going about my day covered in blood."

He shrugged. "You care for your people. An admirable trait many leaders do not possess. Not enough, at least, to bother dirtying their hands for."

Kartek ducked her head at the compliment, but he spoke again before she could think of something to say.

"What is all this?"

"As our vows were somewhat . . . rushed, I thought it might be beneficial for us to spend some time getting to know one another."

"A pleasant prospect." But the sudden wariness in his eyes told her he thought such a suggestion sounded anything but pleasant.

"Perhaps we could walk first. The food is still rather hot."

He nodded, and Kartek tried to calm her frantic heart as they began their walk. She wasn't ready to make the decision about the wine. Not yet.

They didn't speak at first, other than for Kartek to point out various features of the palace, such as the gardens and the various courtyards, the scroll room and the kitchens, until they made their way up to a tower that was open on all sides.

"This is my favorite place in the whole palace," Kartek said as they gazed out over the valley behind the palace. Hedged in by the distant mountains, visible on every side, the farming fields, fields for chattel, river, and sand dunes filled the valley.

Rich reds, browns, oranges, yellows, blues, and even a few shades of green made the scene look much like one of the mosaics in the palace's entryway. If only her heart could be so peaceful. After a moment of silence, she finally was able to raise her eyes to his.

To her surprise, his large green eyes were already fixed on her face. But unlike the day before, she no longer found them disconcerting. Only . . . wishful. And though his skinny, pale limbs certainly weren't the kind that would make women giggle, such as Gahiji's had been, they no longer seemed quite so repulsive.

What was wrong with her? She needed to focus!

"What are those green places over there?" he asked, pointing.

"There is a river that runs lower in the valley, the one the enchantress was encamped at farther down, actually, and it floods each season, allowing us to grow crops nearby. Flax, wheat, barley, even different kinds of fruits and figs."

"You wouldn't know such things would grow in this desert." He turned slowly to look at the rest of the valley. "The first time I saw your palace, I'd never seen so much sand in my life."

An opportunity. "If you didn't grow up with this much sand," she tried to sound nonchalant, "where are you from?"

"We were in the desert as well, but there was a bit more greenery, as our desert bordered the sea."

"Aren't the Ibhari nomadic?"

"Yes," he said, "but they have preferences. All tribes do. It is part of the reason we don't kill one another each time we cross paths."

In her head, Kartek tried to list the number of kingdoms and tribal regions that on the coast, but she had never excelled at geography. But really, did it matter? He had already told them he was part of the Ibhari tribe, and no one in that camp had even known he existed. "So where are you from then?"

"I told you my father's tribe was the Ibhari." He took a deep breath. "But my mother was from the north."

So that would explain his pale skin, though it still didn't answer her question. "But where are *you* from?" She crossed her arms. "Ahmos said that when asked, no one in the Ibhari tribe had ever even heard of you."

"Is it important?"

She lifted her chin a little. "I think it is."

He frowned, his dark brows pulling down over his thin face like thunderclouds. "And why is that?"

She let out a strangled laugh. "I married you and made you emeeri over my people! And yet you think it strange when I want to get to know you?" She gestured at the nearest window in the direction of the healing tents. "Not to mention that you can apparently put tribesmen to sleep while they're in the middle of killing someone! So yes, I would like to get to know you better. And knowing you means knowing about you."

"No, you're not trying to get to know me." He turned and stalked back down the tower steps, taking them two at a time.

She gathered her purple skirts and ran after him, but it was impossible to run and look dignified at the same time. "What do you mean?" she called over his shoulder. "I'm asking questions, aren't I?"

He swerved and glared down at her. "No, you're asking for facts, details anyone who knew me might give. How much have you truly tried to learn about *me*?"

"I haven't had the time! We've been married one day!"

"But you could at least try to learn without assuming you already know the answer! Where I am from does not define me. What order I am in the birth line and the name of my father's tribe does not make me who I am."

She wouldn't have thought it the day before, but now she

could see that in his anger, her new husband was quite capable of looking dangerous.

He stepped closer. "You are so determined to judge me that you refuse to look any farther than your own preconceived notions and beliefs."

She glowered up at him, indignation and guilt warring inside her. "Can you expect me to do otherwise? When the bride hardly has a say in the matter—"

"Jahira." Ebo stepped out from the shadows. His hand rested on his sword, and he stared hard at Dakarai. "Are you being troubled?"

She took a deep breath and closed her eyes. "Ebo, I am fine."

He took a step closer. "You are confident, Jahira?"

"Yes." She returned her husband's glare. "I suggest," she said icily, "that we continue this conversation in the privacy of my room."

"*Your* room?"

"Our room! Whatever you wish to call it. But I do not wish to air our dispute here in the public eye!"

Dakarai eyed her angry bodyguard before whirling around and marching forward, not slowing so that she might keep up or walk beside him.

She did her best to look dignified as she hurried forward, but inside, Kartek felt like a dust storm had blown her world into chaos. *I am only doing what was asked of me!* she cried out to the Maker. *I am trying to keep my people safe!* Still, despite the confidence she knew she ought to have in her answers to these questions, a small annoying voice inside nagged.

Was he right? Was she judging him unfairly?

As soon as they were back in the room with the door closed, he pushed himself up against the far wall and rubbed his eyes with his hands. "This is all wrong," he muttered. "None of this was supposed to happen."

"That!" she cried out, flinging her sandals down beside the door. "It's words like that that make me ask such questions! You obviously planned something in coming here! You didn't happen upon me by accident at that well!" She put her hands on her hips. "Only a handful of people even know that well exists, let alone that I like to go there."

"I didn't know that you like to go there . . . It was only a hunch."

"A hunch?"

"You like lotus flowers. I thought there might be some on the outskirts of the palace."

She blinked at him, the words she'd planned to spit out melting away on her tongue. "How do you know that? Either of those things?"

He looked down at his hands. "You were out once with Rayis Gahiji."

He had seen her with Gahiji?

"You were visiting him and his family. I saw you steal away from your group and make your way down to a nearby stream. You stopped at the bottom and picked a wild lotus flower." His voice lowered, no longer a shout. "You smiled at it as though it were your friend. You hadn't smiled that way at anyone else the entire day."

"How do you know all this?" Kartek searched her memory. She had spent little time with Gahiji. There could only have been seven or eight such meetings between their families, and she was sure she had never seen Dakarai at any of them.

"Your betrothed liked to choose public places where he could show off his bride-to-be. Not that he paid much heed to you when you were actually there." He shrugged again and stared at the ground. "Anyone watching could have noticed such things."

Kartek felt her mouth fall open. Had she noticed such things? He was right in one sense, at least, for in the few times they were together with their respective parties full of siblings, cousins, friends, handmaidens, eunuchs, and servants, Gahiji had dragged them all around, whether it was his camp or her kingdom that they were visiting. Everywhere they went, he had wanted to explore the region and find its finest sights and sounds, food and fun. She could still recall his explosive laughter, the kind that got everyone around him to laugh as well. But had he ever noticed her steal away when she needed a few moments apart from the merrymaking and revelry? Had he ever sought to join her?

Not that she could remember. Not that this observer could either, apparently.

"So . . ." She struggled to maintain an authoritative tone. "I have seen you before then."

"In a way." A sad smile lifted his thin pale lips. "But I doubt you noticed—Wait, what's that smell?" He left the wall and sniffed the air, walking slowly until he reached the food where it had been set on the floor. He bent and lifted one of the goblets. He sniffed it again before turning to her, his eyes wide. "You would give me Ebit root?"

Kartek closed her eyes. "I didn't put it there."

"But you knew."

When she opened her eyes again, his face was twisted and he gripped the goblet's stem so tightly his knuckle bones showed through his skin.

"You, of all people, a healer! You knew what poison this is and you allowed them to leave it on my plate?"

"I didn't want to!" Her voice sounded strangled. "I wanted to simply ask you the truth! But you've danced around the truth the entire time you've been here!" She forced her hands to stop shaking and glared at him, willing the guilt to subside.

"But you know how dangerous this is! I could have died!"

"You have sisters!" she shouted. "Would you want one of them to live through what I have been through? To be forced into wedlock? Into giving her people to a man she doesn't know? To share a bed with a man against her will—"

"And it killed me to do so!" He threw the goblet down. It clanged as it hit the floor. "If there had been another path, I would have chosen it in a heartbeat!"

"Dakarai, I—"

"You cannot understand the loathing I hold for myself every time I see you! Because yes, I imagine my little sisters and what kind of monster I would assume the man to be who could have done such a thing to them!" He strode over to where she was standing. She flinched, but he didn't touch her, only stared down with a mixture of rage and anguish. "I came here because someone took everything from me, and when I came, I knew I could be killed . . . or worse, for making such a suggestion as I did."

"Then why did you come?"

"Because I love you. And I couldn't bear to see everything stolen from you the way it was from me."

Kartek fell back a step. "You what?"

"Judge me for it. Call me the monster I am! I deserve it. But if you know nothing else, know this." He strode forward and leaned down until their noses were almost touching, and for the shortest second, she wondered if he would touch his lips to hers. "I have loved you since the day I first laid eyes on you." He brought a hand up and brushed the back of his fingers against her jaw.

She shuddered, but it wasn't from disgust or fear.

"I think you are beautiful and intelligent and everything a man could ever want in a woman."

Her breath was coming so fast Kartek thought she might pass out.

"Dealing with you as I did went against everything I know or believe in," his voice dropped to a whisper. "But telling you what you want to know wasn't allowed yesterday, and it won't be until you uphold your end of the bargain."

She stared at him incredulously. "You have slept in my bed, shared my meals, and we kissed at our wedding. What part have I withheld?"

He fixed her with a dark smile. "That's just it. You've given all you are capable of! But it will never be enough until ... I just wish I could—" He stopped and struggled, as though he couldn't find the words. After a long moment of silence, he turned and ran his hand through his hair with a groan, then took a deep breath. When he spoke again, his voice was low and controlled. "As much as I wish I could spare you the pain of our actions, it's impossible to go back and change anything now." With that, his green eyes clouded over, and clenching his jaw, he turned and stomped out the door.

CHAPTER 9
QUESTIONABLE DUTY

Unable to eat after he had gone, Kartek sent the supper away. She put on her night dress and went to sit on her window seat, pulling her legs up beneath her chin and staring out at the moonlit landscape below. Twice there was a knock at the door, and both times her heart leapt into her throat. But the first was only the servant come to take the food, and the other was another servant to tell her that Commander Fadil's captain was taking all able-bodied warriors with him to Maisef, with the exception of the contingent remaining to protect the palace.

"What shall I tell him in return, Jahira?"

"Tell Ahmos to move the people out of the city as best he can," she replied without turning. "Flee to the west if possible. Hide if they can't."

The servant paused. "Of course, Jahira. But . . ."

"Yes?"

"If . . . if I may be so bold, the enchantress isn't here yet, nor has she made known any intention of coming. Do you think she will really come here next? I mean, we are not a large city. Mightn't she go to a larger one such as Shapina?"

"Nothing is for sure. Now go do as I say."

The moon rose higher over the valley, but Dakarai didn't return. Why did that bother her so much? He hadn't really any right to be angry, not after what he'd done to her. He was the one who had forced her to marry against her will, after all.

She sighed and moved from one window to another, but it didn't unseat the guilt that sat like a rock in her gut. That excuse for her anger, blaming him for everything, was feeling used up, even for her. There was clearly much going on that she didn't understand.

That Ahmos was right and the enchantress was involved somehow with Dakarai's appearance, Kartek had no doubt. Still, she had looked for a sign of artifice in Darkarai's face. Her father, after all, had taught her well how to discern deceitfulness. But she hadn't been able to find any. There had been no unwillingness to look at her. He'd made eye contact repeatedly, even searching her face as though she knew the truth as well as he. No strange pauses, no throat clearing or touching of his nose or face. And whenever he had hidden his eyes, it had seemed to be out of shame more than anything else.

When he had touched *her* face, however . . . desire had taken her by surprise, radiating out from his fingertips to the rest of her body like the scorching rays of the noontime sun. And though she was loath to admit it, she had wanted him to kiss her. Badly. To take her face in his hands and hold her close.

The desire was disorienting. She hated Dakarai. She wanted him gone and to simply have the quiet stillness of her rooms to herself once more, a place where she could retire and rejuvenate her senses in those few precious moments that she wasn't healing, having meetings, hearing citizens' requests, or making grand decisions about politics and people.

"Jahira?" someone called through the door.

She sighed and pulled a dressing gown over her night dress. "Come in, Ahmos."

Ahmos walked in followed by Ebo, who stationed himself just inside the door, hands folded, eyes staring straight ahead as always.

"I wouldn't have intruded, but I saw your husband pacing the halls." Ahmos paused. "From the look on his face I'm not supposing that the supper went well?"

Kartek groaned. "I've made a mess of things." Her head snapped up. "But let Alder Bennu know that her seat in the Alder's Circle will be coming to a swift end."

"What did she do?"

"She did as I asked and did not use Mahat root in his drink." Kartek glared at the place on the floor where the offending tray had been.

"Oh?"

"She used Ebit root instead."

"Oh. I see." He rubbed his shiny head before clasping his hands behind him. "That is a grave misstep indeed. I don't think the other alders will have any problem dismissing her at once. They might be your equal as a whole, but no single alder has the authority to challenge or overstep you outright." He paused and caught her eye. "But how are you, my dear?"

Kartek threw herself back on the window seat. "I've muddled everything. Bennu might have put the Ebit in his wine, but I . . ." She shook her head. "I allowed it to stay. And to make matters worse, I fear my husband may actually be in the right."

"And what makes you say that?"

"He . . . he seems upset about the marriage. He keeps saying it wasn't his choice and he wishes he could have done things differently, but he couldn't."

"Jahira, please forgive my interruption if the advice is not wanted, but it might be easy for him to—"

"He saw me, Ahmos."

Ahmos frowned and looked her up and down. "And I can see you before me now. What do you mean?"

"I mean, he's seen me before, apparently while I was out with Gahiji."

"That would have been over a year ago at least." Ahmos tapped his chin.

"I don't mean he merely looked at me," she said, playing with a piece of her hair. "I mean he *saw* me. He noticed things about me that I had failed to recognize."

"Which would be?"

She shook her head. "I don't know. That Gahiji wished for others to notice me, but never truly tried to get to know me himself. Dakarai, however, was close enough to observe that I prefer to stay away from large crowds, and that I like lotus flowers." She paused. "I do not wish to speak ill of the dead, but . . . Dakarai seems to know me better than Gahiji ever wanted to."

Ahmos walked over to where Dakarai's wine had spilled and bent to mop up the sticky remnants with a cloth he pulled from his belt. "Your parents betrothed you to Gahiji, and he met you himself eight times. I can only suppose he believed your attachment secure enough not to have needed such attentions. Not that such wasn't shortsighted thinking, of course." He stopped and studied her. "You feel guilty, don't you?"

"I know we must proceed with Hedjet's good in mind, but . . . what if he's right, Ahmos? What if Dakarai is truly the victim of wrongdoing just as we are becoming victims now? Might not the enchantress have cursed him in some way as well? Or couldn't he be under some sort of exaction from a more powerful warlord or tribesman?"

"These are all possibilities. But what if he's lying? You have been graced with good men to surround you all your life, but there are many in this world who gain their fortunes making up falsehoods with more confidence than you or I tell the truth."

Kartek traced the beads on her night slippers. "I wish to do the right thing," she whispered.

Ahmos placed a strong hand on her shoulder. "As do I." Then he sighed. "We prayed to the Maker for a miracle. Perhaps this boy is the answer and perhaps not. We must also pray now for wisdom."

"But how will—"

"The Maker wishes for us to be just. Ask the Maker tonight to show you the way, and I will do the same. He will not ignore our cries. Eventually, we will learn the truth, for the darkness cannot hide its nature forever. Now," he squeezed her shoulder and walked to the door. "I suggest you get some sleep. Do not worry about your husband. I will find him and explain Bennu's poor choice of disobedience."

Kartek wanted to wait up for Dakarai, but she found herself nodding in acquiescence. If there was another battle tomorrow, she would need her strength to heal as many men as possible. She would have to leave Dakarai to the Maker.

KARTEK VACILLATED between sleep and wakefulness until sometime later that night when she heard him enter. She stiffened as he got into the bed, but as he'd done the night before, he lay down at the head, making sure they weren't touching.

In a way, that hurt worse than his silence.

She slept in fitful bursts throughout the remainder of the night, but when she awakened the next morning, he was already gone again. Kartek dressed quickly but allowed a handmaiden to assist her this time. She got the feeling this would be a bloody day, and she needed her hair and clothes to be tied up properly so she might move readily when called upon.

The day was already hot as she made her way to the tents. Kartek slowed a bit, however, when she rounded the corner to pass by the tribes' children. As he had been the day before, Dakarai was there. This time he was telling them stories. Unlike the day before, however, he refused to look up even when she purposefully altered her path to walk nearer to them. A single flick of his eyes, and she knew he wouldn't be raising them toward her again. His jaw was suddenly strained, and he leaned forward so he could only look at the children.

All of her guilt went up in smoke, and her annoyance was rekindled. If that's the way he wanted it, then Kartek could play that game too. And she could win. The Hedjet matriarchy was not known for its willfulness for nothing.

To know the enchantress was approaching Kartek's city would have been bad, but to be kept guessing was possibly worse. To prevent herself from going mad, Kartek set about with Nuri and her girls preparing the healing supplies in advance. Salves, powders, bandage wraps, and all their little utensils were gathered, mashed, mixed, and organized in earthen bowls on their wooden carts. Most of the cots were empty by now, as the majority of the men were well enough to have either rejoined their ranks or to have returned to their families to finish healing.

"Are you the queen?" a little voice asked in a thick accent.

Kartek looked over to her left to find a pair of big brown eyes staring up at her. "Here I am called Jahira, but yes, I can also be called the queen. What is your name?"

The girl peeked over the edge of the cart at Kartek's assortment of clay bowls and jars. "I am Lupe. Is that man your husband?" She pointed a chubby finger at Dakarai.

"Yes." Kartek pounded the powder in the pestle a little harder.

"Why are you angry with each other?"

Kartek stopped grinding and peered at the child.

She was young, couldn't be more than six. Her mouth was sticky with what looked to be the remnants of a date, and her dress, which was too short, was dirty and torn in several places.

"Where are you from?" Kartek asked.

But the child shook her head. "I don't know why you don't talk to him more. He is kind."

"Little one, I don't see how that's any of your—"

"My daddy was hurt in the battle." Lupe started to skip in a circle, all the while staring at the sky. It made Kartek dizzy just to watch. "But he," the girl pointed at Dakarai again, "sang my daddy a song that made him feel better."

"And what song would that be?"

The little girl shrugged and continued skipping. "I don't know. But it helped my daddy sleep."

Unbidden, the tribal head's words echoed in Kartek's mind. *But only the true Rayis's song is strong enough to command us all.*

Kartek had a sudden flash of inspiration. "Did he whisper the song?"

But the little girl wasn't listening anymore. Instead, she was skipping away.

"Here" Kartek waved at the nearest servant she could find. "I need two things from you."

"Of course, Jahira."

"First, I need to find Ahmos. Second, find an alder and have him request to speak with the tribal leaders. It's urgent." She paused. "Tell them it's about the Warrior's Song."

CHAPTER 10

OTHER METHODS

I am very sorry, Jahira," the manservant said, trotting up to her and offering a quick bow. "I have looked all over the palace, but it appears Alder Ahmos was seen leaving this morning and no one knows where he went. Would you like for us to send out word you wish to speak with him now?"

Kartek pursed her lips. "No, I will speak with him later. Just notify me when he returns to the palace." She paused. "Any news from the tribal leaders?"

The servant looked at his feet. "I am sorry, Jahira, but none of them wish to discuss the song further with you. They said it is sacred, and not for . . ." he glanced up at her, "outsiders."

So that was the game they were going to play. Kartek balled her fists up in her thin skirts. For people who boasted of their bravery with weapons, they were too cowardly to rouse her ire themselves. She would just have to locate another source of information. "Then find me Oni," she said.

As soon as Oni had joined her, Kartek set off for the outdoor spring, the one where she had talked with Ahmos the day before.

The walk along the outside wall wasn't far, but it was just a long enough distance from the tents for Kartek to think.

"What exactly," Oni panted as she half ran to keep up with Kartek's determined pace, "are we looking for at the outer springs?"

"I need to know about something called the Warrior Song."

"I have never heard of such a thing."

Kartek shook her head. "I hadn't either until Gahiji's death. Which is why we're going to find out about it." She glanced over at her handmaiden. "I know that look. What is it?"

Oni's face reddened. "It is nothing."

But Kartek stopped beneath the shade of a palm tree. "We have known one another too long to keep such secrets."

Oni's blush deepened and a small smile played on her lips. "It is only . . . I was wondering what it is like to be married," she said in a rush, staring at the ground. "I saw your supper being prepared last night, and I thought . . ."

"Ah," Kartek said in a softer voice. "You are thinking of Waqi."

Oni blushed, and Kartek gave a dry chuckle.

"Unfortunately, I cannot answer it well for I wouldn't know." She heard her friend's gasp, but kept her eyes on the outer pools as they approached them. "You don't approve?"

"No. I mean, I am only . . ."

"Only what?"

Oni paused. "Surprised."

"It is surprising to you that I am not close to the man I've known for only two days?"

"No," Oni said slowly. "That is not surprising. I am only surprised because he seems such a kind soul, and you are such a kind soul . . . if I am not too bold. After meeting him I only assumed that you would . . ." She snuck a glance up at Kartek. "I believed you might be happy."

Kartek frowned and drew her scarf over her face as the glaring sun continued to grow hotter. "So you are thoroughly convinced of his character then? After only a few days?"

"I cannot see into his heart as the Maker can," Oni said, pulling two honey cakes from her little bag and handing one to Kartek. "But I can see what he does."

"And what has he done to earn such approval?" When she got no answer, Kartek glanced back at Oni. "Truly," she softened her voice. "You have ever only been a faithful friend to me. I value your opinion more than you know."

"Well," Oni chewed her own honey cake thoughtfully, "both mornings he rose before I was able to bring your breakfast from the kitchens, no matter how fast I walked. And when I reached your room to leave the food, he simply wrapped his up in a cloth and left. My brother says he saw him bring it down to the children to share it with them. And every day when he is finished playing with the children, he walks among the tribes and talks to the families there." She frowned a little. "He also has an uncanny ability to calm the tribesmen when they get angry."

"I noticed that. Do you know how he does that or what he speaks of?" Kartek stopped at the side of the oasis spring and found a place to wedge them in at its edge. The spring was surrounded by women and children, the mothers gathering water to wash with while the children ran about and splashed one another. Kartek dipped her hands in, bringing the water up to her face. At first she had been in a hurry to find someone to speak with, but this conversation with Oni was becoming far more telling than she had expected.

Oni shook her head. "I only know that whenever he speaks to them, they listen."

"That's what I thought." Kartek looked at the goings-on around them. Was he singing the Warrior's Song? Could Dakarai be the new Rayis that the tribal leaders had spoken of? No one had seemed to recognize him, at least in the healing tents, and the tribe he'd claimed as his own had never heard of him. So for him have the blood of all ten tribes seemed unlikely. And yet . . . what else could he be?

"Were you frightened?"

"What?" Kartek looked up.

Oni shyly tucked a piece of dark hair behind her ear. "The prospect of wedding your first betrothed. Did it ever frighten you?"

Kartek blinked, still puzzling over Dakarai's strange behavior. "I . . . I don't know." She stood and began to scan the women for a friendly face, someone who might answer questions. "My parents chose him for me so long ago that I never questioned it."

But as they moved around the circle gathered at the water's edge, Kartek found herself unraveled by Oni's questions. She did her best to push them to the corner of her mind as she approached a woman who looked like she belonged to one of the northernmost tribes.

"Good morning," Kartek said to the woman, who had seated herself on the other side of the pool and was trying to get a small child to drink from a cup.

The woman looked at her. After a moment of staring, her eyes grew wide. "You are Hedjet's jahira, are you not?"

"I am." Kartek seated herself beside the woman, but Oni continued to stand. "I am looking for someone from the Ibhari tribe."

"I am of the Ibhari tribe. What of it?" The woman dipped a headscarf in the large clay pot she had just filled and began to wash it.

Kartek pitched her voice low. "I have a question about one of your traditions."

"Really?" The woman eyed Kartek's fine linen shirt and skirts. "And if I help you, how will I benefit?"

Kartek frowned, but Oni spoke first. "Do you know who owns the water that you and your children are washing with just now?"

The woman glanced at the water then scowled. "I cannot say I will answer, but go ahead and ask."

"I want to know how the Rayis is chosen."

The woman shrugged. "It passes from father to son in the Ibhari tribe."

"But has it always?"

The woman looked startled. After glancing around, she leaned forward and hissed, "Of course it has! And if it wasn't, do you think *I* would know?"

Kartek was surprised by the woman's reaction, but she raised her hand to keep Ebo from intervening. She could feel him hovering in the shadows of the trees behind her. "I think your whole tribe is hiding something. And not just from me. I think you've hidden it from the rest of the tribes as well."

"I will speak of this no longer!" The woman frantically began gathering her jar and clothes and gesturing wildly at the two children running about her feet. "You may ask Jibril."

"Then who—"

A scream ripped through the air behind them. The woman grabbed her children and began to run. The rest of the women were scattering in a panic, shouting for their children. Kartek jumped up from her seat at the edge of the pool, but before she could see what had caused the ruckus, Ebo was blocking her view, his weapon drawn. As he dragged her to the shadow of a palm tree, however, she managed to catch a glimpse of the creature.

"It's a serpent!" Oni breathed.

Indeed, its long scaled body was much like that of a serpent. But unlike any serpents Kartek had ever seen, this creature was nearly as long as a grown man and just as thick, a diamond-shaped head crowning its coiled body. Metallic green and black scales glinted in the sun as it wound itself tightly.

Ebo pressed down on Kartek until she was nearly flat upon the ground.

"What is it?" Oni whimpered.

Kartek tried to loosen Ebo's hand enough to see, but doing so was difficult. "Its head . . ." She squinted through the dust the running crowd was stirring up. She couldn't see well, but the shape of its wide mouth looked oddly familiar. "I think it might be one of the enchantress's creatures!"

As if to confirm her suspicion, the creature lunged forward and back in the blink of an eye. Beneath it lay a young woman, writhing as she clutched her arm where a set of all-too-familiar teeth marks had begun to bleed.

"I need to get to her." Kartek grasped her jewel. It warmed and tingled in her hand even as she spoke.

But Ebo shook his head, pressing her down even harder than she had been before.

"You're going to break my arm." She glared up at him, but he ignored her, so she tried again. "We need to do something!"

As she spoke, the creature's head snapped to the right. Its spindly reptilian hind legs that Kartek hadn't noticed before pushed it right toward the healing tents.

CHAPTER 11

A TASTE

N o!" Kartek shrieked, but it was too late. The creature was half slithering, half rolling faster than she could run. She looked up at Ebo. "You need to let me go!"

But Ebo just shook his head.

"That is an order!" she screamed.

Still, he hesitated. Only when another shriek rang out, this time from one of the tents, did he slowly let go of her arm. She could see in his eyes that obeying this order was the gravest sin imaginable, but she didn't care. People were going to die.

Kartek took off for the young woman lying on the ground. "Hold her down!" she instructed Ebo and Oni. When they had forced the woman to stay still, Kartek closed her eyes and laid one hand across the bite marks, the other grasping her jewel. Focus was hard, however, with all of the screaming and chaos erupting around her. Clenching her teeth, she tried again. Finally, slowly, the warm honey-like sensation moved from her heart beneath the jewel down to her fingers.

As soon as the wounds were closed, Kartek was off again, following the screams, pausing only long enough to shout for Oni to find somewhere to hide. In the back of her mind, she couldn't help wondering why she was running. It would be wiser to wait to heal each victim until the monster had moved on and her warriors could stop it. And yet, she couldn't hide and simply wait for its victims to pile up, suffering in agony all alone wherever the monster had left them.

She could hear Ebo running beside her. Ebo was the best fighter in her army, which was precisely why he had been made her bodyguard. He would know what to do when they caught it. She could stand to the side to make sure she was able to heal anyone it injured as soon as Ebo had destroyed the creature.

But just as it reached the healing tents, it altered course again, disappearing into the rows and rows of tents of the nearest tribe. Kartek slowed. Ebo stepped in front of her, and the look on his face promised he wouldn't be letting her loose again, order or no order.

Green and black flashed in the corner of her eye just before something slammed against her body with sickening force. She flew through the air and landed hard on her side. Her head hit the ground, narrowly missing a pile of sharp stones.

"Under its leg!"

Kartek tried to raise her head at the sound of the familiar voice, but she could barely roll to her side. Why was Dakarai shouting orders?

"I can't reach its leg!" Ahmos's voice yelled back.

And who was singing?

Hands grabbed Kartek by the arms and gently lifted her up. Her vision was still spinning by the time two of her warriors had her upright, but when they tried to take her away, she motioned for them to wait. They shared hesitant looks but waited as she squinted at the brawl before her, trying to clear her head.

Dakarai held a sword, as did Ahmos and Ebo. The three of

them had surrounded the creature, and other warriors were joining them. The creature whipped its head from side to side, striking with its wide set of teeth at anyone that came too near, including Dakarai, who stood close to the creature's tail.

"Try to strike beneath the limbs!" Dakarai called again. "Its scales are softer there!"

Now she knew she was having visions. Soft-spoken, gentle Dakarai, who hardly looked strong enough to hold the sword, let alone wield it, was shouting out the orders. The focus in his face was practiced, and his arms and legs held as ready a stance as any warrior Kartek had ever seen. His pale face was taut as he issued commands again and again. And to her even greater surprise, the others listened, following his instructions as though he had been emeeri for years rather than days.

Kartek was frozen in place as Dakarai slashed at the creature's back scales, and though she couldn't understand why, horror filled her. *Don't let him die*, she prayed without realizing she'd even asked.

Dakarai tucked and rolled out of the way as the serpent turned again to snap at him with its needle-like teeth. But the bite that had been meant for Dakarai was instead delivered to Ahmos. Kartek screamed as the monster sank its teeth into Ahmos's chest and stomach. The men helping her stand tried to hold her back, but they weren't able to contain her. She ran toward Ahmos's limp body as the others turned their efforts toward drawing the beast away from the camp.

But it was too late. By the time she reached Ahmos's side, his breathing was all but gone, and his eyes were closing.

"No." She fell to her knees, grasping his hand in hers. When she reached up for her jewel, however, her hands felt only her bare skin. Frantically, she felt around for the chain, only to realize it was gone.

"My jewel!" she cried out. She wasn't sure who she was even speaking to, as everyone around her was either fleeing or fighting. But she called out just the same. "Help me find my jewel!" Looking back down at Ahmos, she squeezed his hands in hers, closed her eyes, and began to pray. "Please, Maker, let me heal—"

"Keep your power. You will need it for others."

Opening her eyes, she shook her head. "No, Ahmos. I won't let you die."

"Jahira, you have no control over such things." With a shaking hand, he reached up and brushed the tears from her face. "Besides, jahiras do not cry in public."

"I don't care." She placed her hand on the largest of the tooth holes that were now pooling blood all over his stomach. She would heal him. Her mother had said healing without a jewel was possible. So she closed her eyes and waited.

But nothing came. There was no smooth tingling sensation flowing out from her heart. No wispy pink light glowed above the wound. And as each second ticked by without her power, doubt began to creep in as well. After all, how could she hope to heal him without her jewel? With all the distractions, she'd hardly been able to heal the woman a few minutes before, and that had been with her jewel firmly within her grasp.

"Kartek." He cradled her face in the palm of his trembling hand. "I promised your father I would strive to keep you safe and happy until you were a woman. And I am proud to have done that." He removed her hand from his stomach and squeezed it. "I am going now. I can feel it in my bones. There is nothing you can do."

"But I must—"

He coughed violently. As he did, Kartek could vaguely hear the continued sounds of the fight surrounding her, but she no longer cared. Instead, she continued to try and revive him, but any power that might have come felt as though it was swirling uselessly inside her hand rather than moving into his body as it should have. She hadn't struggled like this since . . . well, since her powers had first appeared.

"I do not have the time to tell you how," he wheezed, "but after speaking with the tribal families here, I can assure you that Dakarai is not—"

An ear-piercing screech rang out. Kartek looked up to see the diamond-shaped head hovering above her.

Once again, her body was slammed to the side. But this time, it was Dakarai who had knocked her to the ground.

"I need to help him!" Kartek tried to push him off. "Let me go! He needs me!" As she scrambled to get back to Ahmos, though, Dakarai wrapped his long arms around her and yanked her backward. She kicked and fought him as he continued to drag her toward the palace, but he ignored it all. Just before she rounded the corner, she caught one last glimpse of the creature as it hovered over Ahmos's still body.

"LET GO OF ME!" Kartek continued to fight against Dakarai, but pushing against him was like pushing against a wall. "I need to save him!"

"You need to stay far away from *that*!"

A soldier fumbled to unlock a small door in the city wall. Dakarai pulled her through and slammed it shut behind them.

"No! I need to save Ahmos! I need my jewel!"

"We'll find it later."

"No!" Her voice rose to hysterics. "You don't understand! I can't heal without the jewel!"

But he didn't stop or even slow. He proceeded to drag her toward the palace, where he pulled them through another side door. As soon as they were in her room, she ducked out of his grasp, but he had grabbed her arm again before she could make it back out the door. Taking her by the shoulders, he shoved her up against the wall, pinning her there. "You can't save him!"

"Who are you," she glared at him through wet eyes, "to tell me what I can or cannot do? You know nothing of me or my powers! You know nothing of my people! You just came slinking in as though you could slip into being emeeri—"

"You can't save him because he's already dead!"

"You're just saying that because—"

"Because you have to live!" He gripped her shoulders more tightly, leaning in so that their faces were nearly touching. "I swore to protect you when we took those vows. So that's what I'm doing! And yes, I know you wanted to marry Gahiji. I know he was everything I am not! Stronger, faster, more commanding . . . everything an emeeri should be!" His eyes unexpectedly welled with tears and his voice cracked as he whispered his next words. "But he's gone, Kartek! He's gone, and so is Ahmos!"

Kartek stopped struggling as Dakarai let out a single broken sob.

"What are you talking about?" she whispered. Her fingers clutched his sleeves, no longer fighting but rather clinging, suddenly unable to stand on her own. "Who was Gahiji to you?"

But he just shook his head and continued to weep.

Before she knew what she was doing, Kartek had wrapped her arms around him and buried her face in his neck. She had always been told that jahiras should never cry in the presence of others. But hot tears flowed down her cheeks as well, and for once, she didn't mind. There was something comforting in allowing herself to be broken . . . and to no longer be alone.

CHAPTER 12
TO TRY

Kartek didn't know how long they held one another and cried. At some point after dark, though, she awoke on her sleeping mat. She still wore her dusty, bloodied dress, but someone had drawn the curtains, extinguished the lamps, and washed her hands. How had she gotten here? She didn't even remember falling asleep. In fact, where was she? But when she tried to roll over to look around, she couldn't. Something was pinning her hand to the ground.

Her panic faded, however, when she squinted in the light of the single candle to realize that it was only Dakarai. From the sound of his slow breathing, he was asleep as well. Her panic faded even more when she realized her jewel was once again around her neck.

Her first instinct was to wake him and ask what had happened since Ahmos had died. Had the monster killed anyone else? Was Ebo safe? Had Oni found somewhere safe to hide? And . . . where were they? She didn't think they were in her chambers. The air felt too cool for that. But then, she was too tired to trust her senses completely.

Still, something made her wait. Deep in her bones, she felt the desperate need for a few moments of peace. A few moments without war or blood or danger or suspicion or secrets.

Kartek just needed a few moments to exist.

She would never have imagined it two nights before, but the sensation of having Dakarai in the room with her somehow felt . . . natural. His presence had not only ceased to alarm her but even felt comfortable. Try as she might to search her heart, she could find no trace of fear for the man holding her hand.

What was it that Oni had asked her earlier? If the prospect of marrying Gahiji had ever frightened her? Well, if she was honest with herself here in the dark cushion of the night . . .

Yes. Yes, the thought of marrying Gahiji had frightened her. For though she had trusted her parents implicitly in their choice, there had always been an undertone of danger lurking within the man himself. Her argument with Dakarai the night before seemed to have reawakened memories she'd managed to forget, and as she considered the times she had spent with Gahiji and his family, she wondered at the fact that she hadn't before admitted as much to herself. For as Dakarai had said, Gahiji had always been exactly what an emeeri should be, someone who could unite the ten tribes of the Megal Desert. He had been commanding in a way that demanded the attention of all in the room. When he spoke, people listened. When he raged, people cowered. His muscles had been like those of the men in legends, and his dark eyes had glinted as hard as any diamond.

But now that Dakarai had reminded her of the day she'd stolen away to the river, Kartek could recall wondering if there was any room in such a commanding man for tenderness. Would Gahiji ever look at her with that gentle contemplation with which her father often gazed upon her mother? For whenever she had turned to find Gahiji gazing at her, it was more with a glittering pride, the way a hunter might gloat over his prized trophy.

As the time of their wedding had neared, Kartek had satisfied herself with assurances that he was simply contented with the match. And really, what more could she have asked for? She was getting a husband of renowned strength and skill, one that could command over a thousand men. His leadership skills had been praised throughout the land, and his face and body had often driven young women to giggle as they'd yearned after him for their own.

But now, as Dakarai held her hand, Kartek realized just how much doubt she'd withheld from the world and even from herself. For in all the time they had spent in public or even in supervised private settings, Gahiji had never once offered to simply hold her hand.

Was it possible that perhaps . . . just perhaps, Dakarai, with his sickly pale skin and bony limbs and strange green eyes, might hold something precious that the great Gahiji never had?

"Oh, you're awake." Dakarai's voice was thick with sleep. In the light of the single candle that burned from a sconce on the wall, Kartek could see him freeze as he looked at their hands. "I'm sorry. I didn't mean—"

But Kartek squeezed his hand as he tried to let go. "It's all right. And . . . thank you." She gave him a weak smile in the dark. "It seems I needed it."

"You fainted." Dakarai sat up and rubbed his eyes with his free hand. "Oni said something about you not eating enough. I . . . I wasn't sure what to do, so I called a local healer."

Kartek let out a humorless laugh. "That must have surprised him a bit. I've never needed to see a physician in my life."

"He was more than a bit surprised. He was almost too terrified to even look at you. But after talking to Oni and a few of the other servants, he said you simply needed food and rest." Dakarai paused. "You've been pushing yourself too hard over the last few days."

"I haven't had much choice." She swallowed and closed her eyes. "What happened? And how did I get my necklace back?"

"One of the children found it after the fight. It seems the creature broke the chain when it struck you."

Kartek couldn't speak for a moment. She could only thank the Maker as she squeezed the jewel in her hand one more time. Her joy dissipated, however, as he went on.

"Two more men died, unfortunately, before Ebo was able to kill the beast."

"Were any more bitten?"

"No, but . . ." His voice trailed off into the empty darkness.

"But what?" Kartek took her hand back to run it through her hair. Oni must have loosed it, for it cascaded down her shoulders and back.

He stared at his empty hand. "We still haven't had any word from Commander Fadil. Not even a smoke signal."

"I need to go." Kartek began to untangle herself from her blanket, but Dakarai placed a hand on her wrist.

"And what will you do? It is late, and Fadil has most of your men and those of the tribes."

"I will summon the alders. They will help me decide what to do."

"I met with them while you were sleeping," Dakarai said quietly, not looking at her.

"You did?" She frowned. "Why didn't you wake me?"

"The physician was examining you, and the alders wished to meet immediately." He shifted in the bed, looking uncomfortable. "They requested that I join them, as I am now the emeeri."

Kartek thought about this. Her initial reaction was anger,

frustration at being replaced. But what he said was true. Planned or not, he was her husband, and he was now emeeri. It was just as much his place as hers to meet with the alders in a time of need.

"So . . . what did they say?"

"We had the city evacuated as well as we could. Then we sent out the warriors to help the remaining people hide."

"Why?" She looked around once again, her eyes now better adjusted to the dark. Though the sleeping mat beneath her was familiar, the room they occupied was small. It couldn't have been even as large as Kartek's dressing room. There was no furniture inside, nor were there windows. "Where are we?"

He paused. Even in the darkness, she could see the reluctance in his face. "I believe the enchantress has most likely beaten Commander Fadil. And I believe she will come here next."

"What makes you think that?" Kartek did her best to sound confident and rational, but in her head, she felt as though one of the giant desert sandstorms was starting to whip up all around her, blowing up the dust and shredding her reality to pieces, leaving nothing but dirty chaos in its wake. "This has something to do with the Warrior Song, doesn't it? The enchantress coming here, I mean."

His head snapped up from whatever he was examining on the mat. "How do you know about the Warrior Song?"

"One of the tribal heads first spoke of it. Then a child at the tents told me you've been singing to the warriors, not whispering as I'd believed." She paused, sifting through the fuzzy memory of Ahmos's final moments. "And you were singing during the fight weren't you?"

He stared at her for a long time. "The child spoke truth," he finally said in an ancient voice.

A reckless impulse took Kartek by surprise, and she found herself scooting closer so they were face-to-face. "That means that you are the Rayis!" She let out a burst of surprise laughter then clapped her hand over her mouth before letting out a strangled chuckle again. "Jibril has been searching all this time, and there you were—"

"Wait, Jibril told you he didn't know who the next Rayis was?" His voice darkened.

"He said he would need to check bloodlines."

"Oh, how very *considerate* of him."

Kartek thought about asking more about Jibril, particularly considering the acidity of his last comment, but she had more important questions to ask, now that she'd possibly found the salvation of the tribes and her people. "Who are you?" she whispered. "and why won't you just tell me?"

"Kartek, I—"

"I know you're more than you say you are!" She leaned forward and gripped his hand again. "You know too much about me. About the palace!" She gestured to the single door at the end of the room. "About the tribes and the enchantress! If you would only tell me, we might be able to figure this out together!" She leaned forward. "You can sing the Warrior Song! This changes everything!" She ran a hand through her hair, her mind working frantically. "If you have any essence of the song at all, that means you must have some of the bloodline within you! Maybe not to the extent of what Gahiji had, but enough to—"

"It's just as I said last night." He shook his head. "I wish I could tell you. But I can't."

"It surely can't be impossible."

"No, it's not impossible," he said, his green eyes suddenly wary. "But it would require something of you."

Kartek paused, not sure she was ready for any more requirements. But as the seconds passed by, an animal cried out from somewhere beyond the walls around her. The sound was mournful and lonely. Most likely the way Kartek's people were probably feeling right now as they hid and waited for the enchantress to descend.

"If it means telling me everything, then let me know what I must do."

He eyed her carefully. "Anything?"

She nodded, though not without caution and a little bit of fear slithering up within her chest.

He drew in a deep breath. "Kiss me."

"Kiss you?" Kartek blinked. That was all? "I kissed you the night we were wed."

But he shook his head. "That was as good as forced, something you did because it was expected of you. I mean . . . a real kiss. One given of your own free will."

"You mean . . . a kiss of true love?"

He nodded.

The requirement was simple. Really, the simplest thing she'd been asked to do since the tribes had come to her desert valley. And yet . . .

Kartek stood up and walked over to the farthest wall to lean against it. Just like everything else about him, the requirement was so strange. But then, she had kissed him two nights before. Surely she could do it just as easily now. Kisses were simple, weren't they? A man and woman coming together, the lips of one briefly brushing against those of the other. He hadn't said it need be a long kiss.

But a kiss born purely of love?

Did Kartek even know how to love? She had loved her parents, of course. Ahmos. Oni. Even Ebo. But those were different kinds of love, nothing like what this would require of her. How could she kiss Dakarai without knowing how she felt about him and expect it to change anything? If she could remove her heart and examine it, Kartek was sure she would find a massive tangled knot with a thousand different threads. Over the last few days, she had struggled with hatred, anger, confusion, rejection, curiosity, and even a foreign kind of affection. But love? She wasn't even sure if she would know it when she felt it.

"You said yesterday that you loved me," she whispered. "How do you know you love me?"

He was quiet for a moment. "It began as respect," he finally said in a low voice. "But the more I saw you, the more I realized you were consuming my thoughts. I would often wonder how you were spending your days, or if you were sad or happy. I began to think of your welfare more than my own."

"But ever since meeting you—well, being aware of having met you—I've been suspicious, angry, and belligerent toward you, even though you've worked hard to help my people and protect me." She shook her head. "I don't even understand the love you decided to give. How can I expect to give it back when I don't comprehend it?"

"When we look deep into our own hearts, do any of us understand love on our own?" He leaned toward her just a hair. "And yet the Maker gives it."

Kartek turned to face him, a dangerous churning in her stomach. There was no name for the sensation that swirled about inside her now. It certainly wasn't the excited admiration she had once held for Gahiji, nor the intense adoration she'd seen shining in her parents' eyes for one another. But it was something. A desire. She might not love Dakarai passionately now as she'd imagined doing for her husband. But did that necessarily mean she might never know love as she'd hoped?

"I think . . ." she whispered. "I think I would like to try—"

"Break it down!"

Kartek whirled around to look at the door, but Dakarai was

already out of bed and in front of her, his sword drawn. As he held it ready, the door burst open.

A young woman who looked to be near Kartek's age stood on the threshold.

"Marid." Dakarai said the name like a curse.

The young woman merely smiled at him. "It is good to see you again, too."

CHAPTER 13
THE BEST REVENGE

As the stranger spoke, Ebo appeared in the doorway behind her. Splatters of blood covered his arms and face, but he raised his arms, his eyes filled with bloodlust. Before he could strike, a serpentine creature latched its teeth into his shoulder and dragged him out of sight.

Kartek screamed.

"Take them to the throne room," the woman said, turning and walking back out the door.

"This is between us, Marid!" Dakarai shouted as more of the serpent creatures entered the room and surrounded Kartek and Dakarai. "She and her people have nothing to do with our quarrel!"

But the strange woman—Marid as Dakarai had called her—was already gone, gliding out of the room with an air of ease.

"You know the enchantress?" Kartek turned to Dakarai in horror, but before he could answer, he was prodded by one of the horrible diamond-shaped heads toward the door. Another prodded Kartek.

Servants screamed and the few warriors who had been left

behind scrambled to fight the dozens of creatures as they marched Kartek and Dakarai down the halls. But Kartek could only watch in agony as the home she loved so much was ravaged by the monsters, and the people who tried to protect it were punished. She could do nothing to stop it. The monsters' screeches echoed down the halls from every direction. Kartek prayed that Dakarai and the alders had hidden her people better than they had hidden her.

The throne room had always been a place of order and ceremony to Kartek. Even as a child, she'd felt at home in the great hall of white sandstone walls decorated in their colorful frescoes and mosaics. But now the room felt cold and empty as the enchantress took her place in Kartek's seat at its head.

"What do you want?" Kartek shouted as she and Dakarai were forced to their knees before the throne. "You attack my people and my allies, and yet you make no demands?"

But the stranger only fixed her dark almond eyes on Dakarai. "I must congratulate you on making it this far. I really wasn't sure you would survive the heat, particularly at this time of year." She gestured to the windows as though they were merely discussing the weather. "And it seems you not only found someone willing to share her bed, but she's not put you to death yet, either. How did you do it?" The words were spoken casually, but there was a fierce undertone to them.

"I had no choice," Dakarai said though his teeth.

"But you did!" The young woman stood, all patience fleeing her face. She might have been pretty had her scowl not been so deep.

"Killing my family and forcing me into wedlock isn't exactly my idea of a choice," he shot back.

Marid smiled again, though the expression looked even more menacing on her young face than the glare had. "You mean the same way you gave the jahira the choice of marrying you?"

Pain flashed across his thin face, followed by anger. "None of this had to happen. You were the one who decided to begin the violence."

"You were the one who was unfaithful!" Marid screamed. "You abandoned me! And for who? Your cousin's betrothed?"

Kartek turned to stare at Dakarai. His *cousin's* betrothed? Did she mean Gahiji?

Dakarai was shaking his head. "I warned you that if you chose this path, I couldn't follow. I don't know why you were so surprised when I kept my word."

Marid stepped down from the throne, her strides wide and purposeful. "So you chose *her*?" Marid turned to glare at Kartek. "I see nothing extraordinary about her." Flipping her many braids, the seashells and beads woven into them clinking against one another, she walked in a slow circle around Kartek. Then she reached up and fingered Kartek's necklace.

"Don't touch that." Kartek tried to draw back.

"Or what? Legend says that without this jewel, your power is nothing." Marid grasped the jewel and yanked.

Kartek wanted to crumble when she heard the chain snap. Again.

"Well," Marid said as she turned back to Dakarai, still holding the jewel, "what do you have to say for your *gifted* jahira now?"

Dakarai said nothing, but his lips were white as he mashed them together and stared at the wall behind the thrones.

"Well, if you won't talk to me, then I will talk to her." Marid faced Kartek. "They say you are powerful."

Kartek wasn't sure how to respond, so she did as Dakarai and stayed silent.

"Well, are you?"

Kartek leveled her a glare, but before she could consider a smart retort, she began to choke. She gasped as she reached up to find one of the serpents had wrapped the end of its tail around her neck.

"Stop!" Dakarai shouted. "I'll tell you what you want, just stop!"

The scaly tail released her throat, and Kartek fell forward, wheezing.

"I thought that might end your silence." Marid dusted her hands as though she'd dirtied them. "Then tell me, *Dakarai*, why her?"

"My answer is the same as it always was."

"Your answer wasn't satisfactory."

"How much simpler can I make it?" Dakarai shouted. "Take one look at the monstrosities holding us captive, and you might get an inkling of an idea!"

Marid scoffed. "It was never about them."

"You're right. It wasn't. It was about the change that came over you when you decided to pursue power that should never have been yours! It was about the way you tried to control others around you." His green eyes flashed. "The way you tried to control me."

"I did it for us!" Marid fell to her knees before him and reached out to touch his face.

For some reason, this small action angered Kartek more than she would have expected.

"Your father saw you as nothing!" Marid said, her voice suddenly a whisper. "They treated you as nothing, trading you for a child that wasn't their own! They stole your birthright! I only ensured that Gahiji could no longer steal your glory or your rightful place!"

"What rightful place?" Kartek asked, her voice shaking more than it should.

Before Dakarai could answer, Marid had turned and slapped Kartek in the face before moving back to him. "I gave you the world, but you chose to come crawling here to her!"

"How could you think I wanted Gahiji dead?" Dakarai cried out. "I loved him!"

"He was holding you back! They all were!"

"*You* were holding me back!"

Marid flinched as though she had been the one slapped.

That was when Kartek saw the war for what it was. The bloodshed had never been about land or fealty or even Kartek's priceless jewel or abilities. It had been about Dakarai all along.

Kartek studied him once again, desperately trying to find some feature that she could place. He had obviously seen her often enough before. If the enchantress was to be trusted, this was Gahiji's cousin. But what did that have to do with a birthright or stolen glory?

Dakarai's acidic words interrupted her thoughts. "Birthright or none, the day you chose to embrace the darkness, I told you that every piece of your power would come at a cost." His green eyes were rimmed red. "That cost was me. And you knew it. And you still chose the darkness!"

Whether the monsters allowed him to or whether Marid was too distraught to control them, Kartek couldn't tell, but he finally rose from his knees and looked down upon the young woman with a sneer. "You asked why I chose her?" He spat on the ground at her feet. "Because she is everything you are not. Where you break, she mends. Where you suppress, she lifts up." He leaned forward. "You seek glory. She seeks to heal."

Marid stood, too. "You stand there and judge me all you want," she said with a shaking voice. "But we did the same thing, you know. I wanted you. You wanted her." She lifted her chin higher. "We both went for the objects of our desires."

"Not until you killed my family." Dakarai shook his head. "Not until you forced my hand. And don't pretend you weren't planning to punish her all along."

"I did what I did to give you the place you deserve in this world," Marid said, lowering her eyes to the ground. Her voice was hardly above a whisper. "You were always the good one. You saw those who were beneath you, and you never stooped to pride or pomposity even though they had all betrayed you. But it seems I was mistaken. You are every bit as ungrateful as Gahiji ever was." She finally brought her large brown eyes up to meet his, tears sticking to her long lashes. "I just have one more question. Why did you come to her? Here?" She gestured at the walls surrounding them, her movements growing frantic and quick. "You knew I would follow you. Why not go somewhere I couldn't find you?"

"Because I knew that no matter what happened to me, you would be jealous. And you would go after her no matter where I was." Then, for the first time since being dragged into the room, Dakarai met Kartek's gaze. His eyes were large and pleading. "I only wanted to keep you safe," he whispered. "I never meant for things to come to this."

Marid came to stand before Karate and raised the dagger.

Time stood still as Kartek shut her eyes and waited for the final blow. But when she begged the Maker to make her death quick, she felt no pain. Instead, a cry went up and a body landed on her lap. Opening her eyes, she looked down to find Dakarai stretched across her legs.

Marid was staring at him open-mouthed with a look of horror, and only then did Kartek realize the blade that was meant for her was buried deep in Dakarai's chest.

CHAPTER 14
A DIFFERENT MAN

N o!" Kartek screamed. She bent over him. A familiar pain filled her with an intensity she hadn't felt since losing her parents. Why it was there, she couldn't say. Only the piercing knowledge that she needed to save him. That without him, her heart would rip in two.

Whoever Dakarai was, he hadn't come to hurt her. She could see that now as plain as the man lying before her. He had come out of a sense of duty. He had spoken the truth all along, swearing that he meant her no harm. Somehow, he had fallen in love with her long before that. And somehow, without even knowing it, she had begun to do the same with him along the way.

Kartek sobbed as she pulled out the knife and pressed her hands over his chest. But the blood continued to gush, and though she could feel her power flicker in and out of her fingers, she could not heal him. He tried to raise a shaking hand to her face, but she pushed his arm back down and touched her fingers to his mouth. "Don't," she whispered. "Save your strength!" Then she remembered that Marid had taken her jewel.

"Please!" she called up to the enchantress as she pressed his hands over his chest. "Let me heal him!"

But Marid didn't seem to even hear her. She only stood there, motionless, Kartek's jewel nowhere in sight. Kartek considered attacking Marid in her stupor, but then realized that powers such as Marid's could have sent her jewel anywhere. Perhaps even have destroyed it.

Kartek turned back to the wound, praying desperately for the power her mother had spoken of. But the pink haze that floated above her hands as she worked only flickered a few more times before dissipating completely. "No!" She clenched her jaw and tried again. "No, you can't die! Not now, not when I need you!"

No matter how hard she pleaded, though, his eyes started glazing over and the sad smile he'd been trying to summon began to melt away. The thin pale cheeks she had despised days before now belonged to the most beautiful face she had ever seen. If only that face would move. Even a twitch would have given her hope.

She turned back to Marid, who still seemed rooted to the spot. "I need my jewel!" Kartek screamed, keeping one hand on the bleeding wound and stretching the other out toward the girl. "Give me the jewel so I can save him!" She tried to catch the enchantress's eye. "I beg you," she whispered.

Still, Marid wouldn't move.

Kartek pressed down on his chest even harder, trying to staunch the blood. But as his face began to lose what little color it had, rebellion streaked through Karate's heart like lightning to dry brush. The enchantress had claimed to love Dakarai, but, it seemed, had killed Gahiji while trying to prove that love. Kartek had sworn to love him when they'd been wed, but had shown him none of that love since.

It was too late for Marid to undo what she had done. But now, as Dakarai's breaths grew more shallow, Kartek had one last chance to make it right.

"I'm sorry," he rasped, running a shaking hand down the side of her face.

"Don't be." And leaning down, she pressed her lips to his.

This kiss was nothing like their first had been. She could feel the life draining from him beneath her bloodied, aching fingers, but there was an earnestness, a simplicity in his mouth and the way his fingers gently gripped her face that changed something within her. She shuddered and fought the sudden desperate desire to laugh and weep and sing as eyes still closed, his hands explored her cheeks, her brow, her jaw. His thumbs wiped away the tears she hadn't realized were falling.

The heat from his mouth pierced her, an arrow to the heart, where it radiated out to the rest of her body like the rays of the midday sun, branching out until her entire being hummed with the sensation. She could feel her fingertips warm. Light the color of a desert sunset glowed beneath them. Gasping, she jumped back as his body began to shimmer.

His pale skin began to deepen until it had warmed to a golden brown. The body that had seemed emaciated and worn began to fill out. Though he was still lean, wiry muscles covered his arms and legs. A chain mail shirt of the finest metal and trousers of the richest red now adorned him in the clothing of only the finest warriors. Weapons of every kind decorated his chest, arms, and belt. But only when a deep breath filled his lungs and he opened his green eyes did Kartek recognize the man she held in her arms.

"Unsu!"

It all made sense. How he had seen her from afar, close enough to know her but overshadowed enough by Gahiji to be invisible. How many hours had she spent in his company and hardly noticed him? And yet he had seen everything about her, things she hadn't even known about herself.

"You . . . you broke my spell," Marid breathed. Then her voice rose to a shout. "You weren't supposed to love him!" As her voice grew, Marid's monsters seemed to come to life again, awaking from the frozen stupor they'd stood in as the enchantress had stared at his broken, spent body moments before.

Kartek hit the ground, but Dakarai—Unsu pulled two weapons from his sash and held them up to the monsters, crossing their blades in a challenge as though to taunt them. Then he raised his face to the ceiling and let out a powerful cry.

It was a song, Kartek realized. One that raised bumps on her arms and made her skin prickle. Even before the first notes ended, however, she could hear them coming. Cries of warriors echoed the song. They could be heard in the halls, outside of the palace, even on its rooftop, drawing nearer with each second.

The monsters swarmed down on him as one, but as they did, Kartek turned to see her own men and those of the tribes descend upon the throne room like bees from every direction.

Marid screamed directions at her creatures, but the louder she shouted, the more she seemed to be losing control. Kartek looked back and forth between where Unsu fought, his lean, graceful body moving in and out and under and around the creatures as though he were dancing, and Marid, where she stood shrieking at her creatures.

Her men might have a chance. If there were enough to keep coming.

But even as she began to hope, the creatures began to grow again in size and strength. Men started to fall all around her, and Kartek felt hope die as she stood there without her jewel, helpless to heal and helpless to fight.

Kartek did not like being helpless.

Whirling around, she grabbed ahold of Marid's dagger. Marid didn't let go, however, and Kartek found herself fighting for her own life as they struggled.

"You think you deserve him!" Marid spoke through her teeth. "You hardly knew he existed!"

"You're right." Kartek dug her heels into the slick stone floor. "A mistake I intend to remedy!" As she spoke, though, her right foot hit a slick spot on the tile and she tumbled backward.

Marid fell on top of her, this time pointing the dagger down at Kartek's chest. "I don't know how you found a way around the curse, but I *am* stronger than you!"

"You think you own him? Like a dog?"

"I know what's best for him!"

A sharp pain hit her hands, and Kartek realized her grip had slipped and she was now clutching the blade. Where her fingers should have run red with blood, however, a soft pink glow surrounded them. Almost immediately, she felt her skin harden where the blade should have cut through.

For the first time, Marid began to look worried. She pressed harder, but that only fueled Kartek's determination. This woman had killed Gahiji, murdered hundreds of warriors, cursed Unsu, and now she had dared to enter Hedjet's sacred court as though she had any right to the throne or its people.

"Hedjet is *my* kingdom," Kartek said, her muscles filling with a new kind of strength. She began to press the knife backward. "That is *my* throne." The swirling pink grew even brighter so that it reflected in Marid's bulging eyes. "This is *my* power."

A movement to her left caught Kartek's eye. She leaned forward and dared to smile. "And that is *my* husband."

As Kartek spoke, Marid turned just in time to see Unsu's arrow. The enchantress's mouth fell open, but she made no sound as her grip slackened and she slumped away from Kartek and onto the floor, taking her knife with her.

A victory cry went up all around, but Kartek let herself fall back onto the floor, panting. She didn't have long to rest, though, for in a moment she'd been swept up into a pair of sturdy arms.

"Are you well?" he breathed into her hair. "Did she hurt you?"

She leaned her head on his shoulder. "I should hope I'm a bit harder to kill than that." She paused, then dared to meet his eyes, and suddenly, she felt incredibly shy. "So . . . Unsu."

He met her gaze unhappily. "Dakarai is my second name." He paused. "It was the only one I was allowed to keep after my parents switched me with my cousin. I'm sorry for the deception."

"No more apologies." Kartek looked around at the battle-ground that had been her throne room. The creatures had all disappeared, but there was far too much carnage and too many injuries to give way to the rush of feelings that were trying to flood her mind and heart. "Let us get this mess cleaned up. Then I think I am entitled to supper and a very long explanation."

She could feel him tense up beneath her. "Of course." He cleared his throat and set her on her feet, stepping back and putting his hands behind his back. He dropped his gaze to the floor. "Where do you wish for me to meet you?"

She reached up and gently took his face in her hands. "In *our* room."

He held her gaze for a long moment before the fear began to melt from his face and a small smile broke through. "Then I will be there."

CHAPTER 15

WHAT IF

Kartek wanted to return to her chambers and collapse on her sleeping mat and stay there for the rest of her days. Or at least a week. Though the daylight was only now beginning to wane, painting the desert in brilliant hues of pink, orange, and gold, she felt as though the day had lasted a lifetime. Instead of venturing inside the room and collapsing, however, she satisfied herself with leaning against the outer doorpost of her chambers and allowing her eyes to close. She reached up and fingered her jewel—which had been discovered on the enchantress's body—glad to once again have its weight on her neck.

After this was over, she was really going to need to find a sturdier chain.

"Jahira," Oni said, touching her shoulder. "You need to rest."

"I will sleep soon enough." Kartek took a deep breath and sat a little straighter. "Where is Alder Cantara?"

"I can fetch her. You just sit for a moment, please."

Kartek nodded her assent and resettled herself more comfortably against her door, Ebo watching closely as she did. For once, his critical gaze was more than welcome. She had feared the worst after he'd been dragged away by the creature, but aside from the first bite, which she'd quickly healed, he had only suffered a few minor cuts and bruises. She closed her eyes and quickly thanked the Maker for his survival once again. After losing Ahmos, she wasn't sure how much more death she could take.

She briefly considered going inside her rooms again and waiting there. Despite her exhaustion, however, she was reluctant to do so. For going anywhere would require standing up, something she was not keen on doing for the next decade or so. To make matters worse, her stomach squirmed in odd ways whenever she thought of her final meeting of the day. The one where she would truly meet her husband for the first time.

"Jahira."

Kartek looked up to find Alder Cantara bowing. She began to stand, but the older woman simply seated herself beside her. "Please forgive my liberty of speech, Jahira," she said, "but you have done more than the work of three today."

Kartek glanced at the familiar medallion the new head alder wore on her chest, and another wave of sadness squeezed her chest. She cleared her throat and tried to speak through it. "Has any word come from Commander Fadil?"

The motherly smile disappeared from Cantara's lined face. "I'm afraid that while some of the warriors survived, he did not."

Kartek began to stand. "I should go to them—"

But Cantara gently took her by the arm and pulled her back down.

And Kartek let her. Unlike Alder Bennu, who always acted as though she should be jahira instead of Kartek, Cantara's words and actions always felt much more like those Kartek's mother might have spoken or made.

"You cannot be in two places at once, Jahira," she said gently. "Nuri has already gone with several caravans of supplies and local physicians to where the surviving men are waiting." She nodded at the window. "You have worked hard today, but those injured here are great in number and will also need you tomorrow. Besides," she gave Kartek a knowing look, "I believe you have an important meeting of another sort tonight."

Kartek swallowed but couldn't get the sudden lump out of her throat. She missed Ahmos so much it hurt. But she needed to talk to someone before she faced the night alone or she might just burst. "I don't understand," she whispered.

"And what would that be?"

"I married him three days ago. He's shared my chambers. We've broken bread together." She frowned. "We even argued and fought. He saved my life and I saved his." She looked up into Cantara's eyes. "So why do I feel so afraid?"

Cantara played with a tassel on her skirt. It was a long moment before she spoke. "You have always been such a conscientious soul." The soft smile melted from her face. "When your parents died, you made taking their places look effortless."

"Oh, but it wasn't!"

"Believe me, I know. But you made it look so, largely because it's your nature to accept burdens without question. I don't know if I should be telling you this . . . but Ahmos and I and several of the other alders would often speak, worrying that you were taking on too much too soon." She gave Kartek a sad smile. "You are only seventeen years. While wise beyond your age, it is unreasonable . . . even wrong to expect you to bear so much on your own. And not to speak poorly of the dead, but we worried that marrying Gahiji under the circumstances of your parents' deaths might make your burden unbearable."

"How so?" Kartek asked.

"He was an efficient leader and never hesitated to ask those around him to do what they could to make his life and reign more productive. And you never learned how to say no."

Kartek's immediate instinct was to defend Gahiji, but she knew deep down that Cantara was right.

"So when we learned that you had made your bargain with Unsu at the well, the alders prayed to the Maker for wisdom. Should we prohibit you from carrying out your word? That would reflect poorly on all of Hedjet and set a bad precedent for your reign. But what if he was a monster or spy? We couldn't allow you to wed your doom. Of course, we didn't know it was Unsu at the time, but after meeting him soon after, I couldn't help wondering if he was an answer to our prayers."

"What do you mean?"

"You thrive on order and predictability. Unsu was unexpected, and your marriage to him spontaneous. Perhaps you are afraid now because you can't predict what he shall do. Unlike Gahiji, he seems to truly wish to take care of you." Her soft brown eyes searched Kartek's thoughtfully. "In the few times I met him, Gahiji never attempted to protect your heart or your interests outside of basic political gain. But Unsu . . . he has done differently from the start." She let out a short laugh. "Forced marriage excluded, of course."

"But I wasn't afraid when I was betrothed to Gahiji . . . not like this," Kartek said. "What if I ruin it? I want . . . I want happiness. I want to love him. But what if I destroy everything?"

"It's strange what undeserved love can do to us." Cantara smiled and stood. "It makes us vulnerable. Vulnerability is frightening. But we all need a soft spot. Even the strongest of emeeris and jahiras need to let someone be their weakness." She began to walk away, but Kartek grabbed her hand.

"Where do I go from here? The people are just now coming

out from hiding. Our warriors are few and many are still recovering." She shrugged weakly. "Even the tribes are without protection."

Cantara reached down and squeezed her hand. "Perhaps instead of charging ahead, you should take life one day at a time. Or better yet, one hour at a time." She glanced up and nodded at the other side of the hall. "Starting with your husband."

CHAPTER 16
ONE HOUR AT A TIME

As Cantara walked away, pausing only to bow to Unsu, Kartek found her stomach tightening anew.

He really was striking in the light of the setting sun. Green eyes glistened like jade, and the contrast of his dark hair with his lightly sun-kissed skin was surprisingly beautiful. Though shorter and much more slender than Gahiji had been, there was a quiet strength about him. Where Gahiji had exuded confidence and superiority, Unsu was watchful and steady.

Kartek wondered now how she hadn't recognized his green eyes from the start. Despite the constant attention she'd paid to her former betrothed, she now recalled admiring Unsu's eyes more than once. He had always been present when she was visiting. It struck her now that she had hardly ever paid him heed. The one time she had paused to compliment his eyes, Gahiji had snorted and replied that such features as Unsu's green eyes and golden skin were simply reminders that marriage to northerners bred nothing but weakness.

Now Unsu stood before her dressed in the clothes of his rightful rank and heritage, signifying his position not only as

Hedjet's emeeri, but as the commander of the ten tribes as well. His dark hair was pulled back into a warrior's tie, and he stood rigid, as though ready to fight at the first sign of danger.

Not that Kartek could blame him. He'd lived through enough danger in the past few days to last a lifetime.

She stood and motioned for him to join her. As soon as they were inside their chambers and the door was shut behind them again, however, the room felt stifling and a thousand times smaller than it had even the day before. Kartek tried to look composed as she sat down on her side of the trays of food and wine that had already been laid out by the servants. After saying a quiet prayer in thanks for the food, they began to eat. The only comfort Kartek found in the silence was that he appeared to feel just as awkward as she did.

This was a wonderful way to start a marriage.

Finally, he cleared his throat. "I suppose I owe you an explanation. I apologize that I will be giving it on the same night that I must go."

Kartek felt her heart fall, though she wasn't sure why. "Go? Are you leaving?"

"Only temporarily." He sighed. "The tribes are gnashing their teeth at one another. They've never been so close for so long. As Rayis, my primary responsibility is to ensure that they don't all kill one another before they can get off in their respective directions." His voice hardened. "I also need to deal with Jibril."

"Jibril? The tribal leader of the Ibhari?"

He nodded unhappily. "Before following you to the well the first time, I tried to find him. He was one of my mother's mentors. Surely, I thought, he would know me even under the curse. But he refused to see me. That's when I knew I would need to go to you."

Kartek recalled her encounters with the older man. Only then did she remember how he had refused to admit that the Rayis had a true living heir. "What will you do to him?"

"The tribes are meticulous in keeping our laws. He suppressed the knowledge of my position, even after Gahiji died."

"But when I asked about another Rayis, some of the other tribal leaders seemed suspicious when he refused to talk about it. Did they know, too?"

"They had their suspicions, but only Jibril knew for sure." Unsu frowned. "The other tribes won't take kindly to that."

Kartek nodded. She didn't need a description of how the tribes would deal with him. The tribes had a Rayis, and she was no longer in charge of their dealings. Only one individual from the Ibhari tribe was her concern now. "That makes sense, I suppose. But," she bit her lip, suddenly feeling as though someone had turned her world upside-down, "when will I see you again?"

He gave her a small smile that warmed her heart and her hopes, though again, she wasn't sure why. "It may not have been an orthodox wedding, but you are now and will always be my wife. I'll send word as soon as peace is restored and it's safe for me to return here." He leaned back a little. "But I can only guess you still have a few questions before I go."

"I admit that I find myself more than a little curious."

He laid his utensils on his plate and studied his food for a long minute before speaking. "I was born on the same night as my cousin Gahiji."

"So he truly is your cousin."

"Oh yes. Otherwise, he wouldn't have had the blood requirements to use the Warrior's Song at all."

"And there is a marked difference between your calls?"

"I am from the more direct line. Mine is stronger."

After hearing the song for herself that morning, Kartek believed it. "Why were you switched with Gahiji then?"

He gave her a wry smile. "Our tribes believe in the Maker, or at least, we claim to do so, but we're also highly superstitious. I was born pale and small compared to other children of our tribe. To say that my father and the other leaders of the Ibhari tribe were disappointed would be an understatement. It was bad luck, they said, to have a Rayis so sickly and light-skinned. No one would follow him. He wouldn't be able to sire children. The tribes would destroy one another, and it would be all his fault." He now glared down at his food, and Kartek had the sudden urge to hug him. "So when Gahiji was born in the same tent, and he was strong and dark..."

"I see." Kartek bit the inside of her cheek. "So how did you find out what they had done?"

"You never met my mother. She died not long after I was born, and my father married again. But from what I can gather, to see me was to see her. And though I didn't remember her, everyone knew that my mother had been a northerner, so it wasn't hard to put the pieces together as I grew older." He paused. "Actually, it was Marid who first encouraged me to find out who I really was."

"So how does she fit into all of this?"

"As children, Marid was my closest friend. We did everything together. It probably wasn't proper, but since Gahiji was the one who would inherit my father's place as Rayis, my . . . parents cared little about how I spent my days. As long as I could fight well enough not to embarrass the family and I knew enough of names and politics not to offend any visiting emissaries, I was allowed to do as I pleased. Though, after I found out who I really was, I did spend a good amount of time trying to watch over my real sisters, though they only thought I was their older cousin, of course."

Kartek frowned at her lentils. "That doesn't seem right."

He shrugged, pushing his own lentils around in their bowl. "It didn't bother me much at first. I had no desire to fill Gahiji's role. And as Marid and I were from the same tribe, as long as I practiced my weaponry enough and stayed out of the way, we were allowed to run free."

As much as she hated to admit it, Kartek was beginning to see why Marid had felt such a strong sense of entitlement to Unsu. She tried to imagine what it must have been like to lose such a close friend, particularly one who had been treated so ill. But she couldn't imagine. Because she'd never had one. Not one her age, at least.

"What happened between you?" She tried to keep her voice unattached and cool. Still, it was hard. What if he still had feelings for Marid after all this time? He had just killed the woman who had professed to love him, the girl he had grown up with. What if he resented Kartek for forcing him into such a position?

He took a long sip of wine. "She began to change. About the time we reached fourteen years, she left with her family to visit an old uncle in the east. They were gone for months. When she returned, she spoke of nothing but this power she had learned from her aunt. When she showed me, I knew immediately that it was dark power." He shook his head. "Our tribes might be infamous for our ferocity and fearlessness, but even we do not allow such dangerous foolishness within our tents."

"I suppose she didn't wish to hear that," Kartek said.

"You could say that. She had always been predisposed to fits of anger or petulance when she didn't get her way, but I, in my naiveté, had always thought it funny and even endearing, as I was often the only one who could coax her out of such tantrums. It made me feel important." He shook his head. "Anyhow, after I told her I would have nothing to do with her newfound powers, she tried to manipulate me into convincing my parents to allow us to marry."

Kartek leaned forward. "Did you?"

"No. Gahiji caught wind of the plot she'd hatched with her friend to put a potion in my drink, and he called them out. It caused a great upheaval within the tribe. Her family was banished."

Kartek wanted desperately to look him in the eyes, but she couldn't raise her gaze from her food. Part of her was dying to ask the question. The other part of her was pleading not to. For some reason, and she couldn't understand why, she felt as though one little word might break her. He had said before that he loved her. But was it true? Or just another part of the ruse? Had the spell forced him to say that as well?

One hour at a time, Cantara had said.

Kartek might need to try one minute at a time first.

"You said . . . you said you loved me," she whispered.

"You mean how could I love you after losing someone like Marid?"

Flushing, she nodded at the ground. So it surprised her when a hand gently cupped her face and lifted it up to meet his eyes.

"I never envied Gahiji anything before I met you. Not strength nor height nor ability nor even stolen birthright. But the day you walked into our tent with your parents, one of my sisters dropped her toy. You picked it up immediately, rather than waiting for a servant to do it. And not only did you hand it to her, you paused to speak with her, brushing the doll off and smiling as you did." Unsu's face darkened and his brows furrowed even deeper. "My cousin barked something at you to reclaim your attention, and for the first time in my life, I resented him. He'd missed the entire moment, the beauty of the little kindness. It wasn't until that moment that I realized how insecure Gahiji really was, despite all he had. And every time you visited after that, I only saw him grow coarser and more possessive of you, as though you were a pretty little doll for him to display to all those who would call on him or visit his domain. He got particularly bad about it after my father and his new wife died and left Gahiji in command."

Kartek sat in silence, unable to move. She had forgotten all about that first meeting with Gahiji. Perhaps she had forgotten on purpose. After all, forgetting was easier than facing the truth that her husband-to-be had fallen far short of her girlhood dream of love.

"But I hardly ever spoke to you," she whispered.

"You didn't have to. What you did was far louder than any of the soft words my cousin ever let you squeeze in edgewise."

Kartek stood and went to her window. She could hear Unsu stand and follow her.

"Marid said she knew you loved me. How would she know that if she was banished?"

"Her family stayed close by. Though they didn't pitch their tent within the camp, they were always within sight, and many times one of them would sneak in and out of the camp to find food. It wouldn't have been hard for her to slip in uninvited while my cousin was holding one of his *audiences* to show you off."

Though Kartek understood the key that such a union would play in the peace of the Megal Desert, she couldn't help but wonder at her parents' choice. Had they held any misgivings after seeing the way he treated her? She had been too young to know any better, but they were too wise not to. What were they thinking? Not as politicians, but as parents?

"Marid approached me several years later and confronted me once when I was alone."

Kartek gathered the courage to look back up at him. This time, Unsu's smile was suddenly shy, and she wondered if he was possibly blushing or if it was simply the sunset reddening his face through the window.

"During your previous visit, you had mentioned to Gahiji that you thought my eyes were striking." He looked down at his hands. "I knew you'd meant nothing personal by it, but the compliment meant the world to me. And Marid had been present long enough to hear it and interpret my reaction. I was pleased, unimportant as the observation had been, and she knew it. After you had gone and I was alone, she came to me and accused me of being in love with you."

"What did you say?" Kartek whispered, not trusting her voice to speak aloud.

"I denied it. He was my cousin, you were his betrothed, and despite his faults, we loved each other like brothers. The last thing I wished to do was steal his bride. But after she left, her accusation continued to haunt me until I could deny it no longer. I had fallen for you over the years of visiting back and forth and seeing you even when you didn't see me. I began to understand what a poor choice for a wife someone like Marid would make, even without the darkness. She still indulged every emotion she felt, and only apologized when it best fit her interests. But you." He lifted his hands hesitantly until they were just touching her arms, making her skin tingle. "You were different."

Kartek's heart beat like a war drum, but she found herself taking a step closer. He gently took her by the shoulders and held her there as though he were touching the finest of glass ornaments, one that might shatter at the smallest breath. And as much as she did feel like a fragile piece of glass, there was also an excitement that bubbled up in the depths of her belly. It made her wish he would pull her closer. That rebel desire wiggled its way into her senses, wanting him to touch her face, her neck. To pull her into the arms she'd fought so hard to stay away from until now.

Gahiji had never awakened such desires within her.

As if he could hear her thoughts, he gingerly reached up with one hand and ran the tips of his fingers down the side of her face.

No. Gahiji had never made her feel like this.

"So what happened next?" she breathed, trying to gain control of her senses once more.

She regretted the question as soon as she'd asked it, for he frowned, and his hands dropped to his sides. Turning back to the window, he folded his arms across his chest. "One of the disadvantages of being cousin to the Rayis is finding that everyone else knows what is best for you, no matter what age you reach. After my parents died, Gahiji decided I would do best to stay behind with the women whenever he took the warriors out to meet the other tribes. Not that I wished to fight, but . . ."

He let out a gusty breath. "I wanted to at least be seen as a man, if nothing else. I think he was also afraid I might not be as weak as everyone had once thought. That's when I began to learn the trade of healing. I was going mad with nothing productive to do." He shook his head. "Anyway, it seemed Marid also knew what was best for me. In her infinite wisdom, she decided that I would be best served by regaining my inheritance through the death of my cousin and younger half-brother. I had been destined for greater things, she told me later, than sitting behind and watching the others gain the glory. So she took it upon herself to alter my situation by killing Gahiji, my younger brother, and the tribe's warriors one day while they were out training for battle."

His voice dropped to a whisper. "They never could have even seen her coming. She blew up a dust storm the equal of which I've never seen. When the dust cleared, her army of monsters was there to assail them."

Kartek felt sick. "Did you see it happen?"

He nodded. "From the door of my tent. They never stood a chance." He frowned. "I'd never tried to use the Warrior's Song before that day. But as I watched her slaughter them, helpless, I knew I would never be so helpless again."

"That's how you knew what to look for when we were attacked in the tents," she said.

"Yes." His voice was hard. "After Gahiji and his men were dead, she came traipsing over to my tent as though she'd done me a favor. She announced that we were now free to marry. I would be leader of the tribes, and we could rule together."

"What did you tell her?"

"That I would rather die."

Without thinking before she did it, Kartek reached out and grasped his hands in hers. "That couldn't have been easy, knowing she had been the one you had once loved."

His expression turned to one of disgust. "It was never real love. Just a boyhood fancy. Once I saw what she really was, there was no way I could ever touch that woman, let alone make her my wife."

"Is that when she—"

"She told me that if I wouldn't have her, she would just have to convince me. Women might wish to have a Rayis, even if he was skinny and pale, but no one would want a nameless vagrant without money or title or family. And to ensure that that was what everyone believed I was, she cast a spell that allowed me to communicate nothing of a personal nature, not anything that could identify me, at least. Then she changed my appearance to make sure no one was able to recognize me."

Kartek sighed. The spell had fooled her sufficiently. She hated being tricked. "But why allow you to leave at all? Why not keep you locked up until you changed your mind or something of that nature?"

He raised a dark eyebrow. "My tribe is not well known for keeping prisoners alive. It's not something we usually even consider. Besides," he shrugged, "she wanted me to see what little I could really do on my own without her. She was sure it would force me to come crawling back, begging for a second chance."

"But why the stipulations, allowing you a chance to escape the curse?"

"Marid lived for fun, and she knew I wouldn't sleep with a woman unless she was my wife. Giving me the requirements of sharing meals, a bed, and a kiss of love meant I was sure to try and sure to fail."

"She wanted to break you."

He sighed and looked at Kartek directly again, his green eyes piercing hers. "I cannot apologize enough for bringing such wrath upon you. If I'd seen her for what she was before we ever got that close—"

Kartek put her fingers up to his lips and gave him a small smile. "You did what you thought was right."

"I knew that even if she didn't find me, she would still come after you. She was too jealous not to. My only prayer as I crawled across the desert to your palace was that the Maker would show me a way to protect you and warn your people. I had seen what she could do, and I thought if I could get here soon enough, I might stop her from doing more if I could only tell you and your commander ahead of time. But I couldn't." He let out a sound of disgust. "In my disguised state, I could barely raise my song above a whisper. Perhaps if I'd practice more before, but . . ."

Kartek took a deep breath and placed her hands on his face, forcing him to look at her. "You did what you could. And," she gave him a half-smile, "it seems the Maker heard your prayers."

His hand found hers, and he turned her fingers against his face. His skin was warm, and its stubble made it rough. "I never meant it to be this way, to trick you into marrying me. But . . . do you think you might one day be able to love me? Maybe when all of this isn't such a shock?"

She slid her hand hesitantly down his face to let it rest on his chest. How could such a simple movement create such a thrill inside her? She took a steadying breath. "When I kissed you, the requirement to break the spell was that it be a kiss of love. The spell is broken now, so it seems I already do in a way." She felt her smile grow shy as she pulled her eyes up to his face again. "It's certainly not the kind of love I ever expected, but . . . I want it to be. I want to know you the way you deserve to be known." She paused. "To love you the way you deserve to be loved."

"I need to go soon. But may . . ." He bit his lip and slowly, slowly put one hand on the small of her back. The other hand cradled her face. "May I?" he breathed.

Wrapping her arms around his neck, Kartek closed the distance between them. Stretching up, she placed her lips on his.

The kiss was gentle at first. But the longer she pressed her mouth against his, the more she wanted. Her heart beat so fast she thought it might take off and fly, leaving the rest of her body behind. His arms tightened around her, and his hand buried itself in her hair.

She could have gone on kissing him forever, but he broke off unexpectedly. Placing his forehead against hers, he kept his eyes closed. "I may be emeeri now, and Rayis, but I don't know where to go from here." His words were breathless, his eyes still scrunched shut. "I don't even know how to be a husband. What if I fail the tribes?" He paused. "What if I fail you?"

Kartek smiled, pulling him down into another kiss. "Why don't we try it the way a wise friend of mine once suggested?"

"Which would be?"

"One hour at a time."

EPILOGUE
PRIORITIES

Kartek reached up to touch the jewel on her forehead once more.

"It's perfectly centered, but it won't stay that way if you keep touching it!" Oni shook her head and smiled as she readjusted Kartek's jewels one more time.

"You wouldn't think I would feel nervous," Kartek said, trying to give her friend a smile.

"Every guest is accounted for and seated," Cantara announced as she walked in. "Jahira, if you keep moving your jewels, they will never lay straight."

Kartek took a deep breath and forced her hands down to her sides where she could finger the fine dress. Somehow, despite the upheaval the enchantress had caused, Ipy had managed to finish all of the adjustments she'd begun the day the tribes had arrived from the desert. A thick gold braid encircled Kartek's waist, and the soft, clean material was finally properly fitted and far more comfortable than the bloodied garment Kartek had worn the first time she'd gotten married.

"I never thought I would get to wear this," she said softly.

"Why do you think Ipy wanted you to have a public ceremony?" Oni gave the seamstress a smug look. "She couldn't bear to have her masterpiece unseen."

"Nonsense." Ipy clucked her tongue as she adjusted the belt again. "This ceremony is for goodwill. My art had nothing to do with it." She gave a small smile. "It will simply make it glorious."

Oni and Cantara stepped back and examined Kartek with critical eyes before Oni came forward and began rearranging her hair, tucking it around the headdress for the fourth time.

"Was this a wise decision?" Kartek asked Cantara, her voice suddenly breathy. The idea of being watched by dozens of the world's most powerful rulers was hardly her idea of an enjoyable afternoon. Being stared at by anybody made her uncomfortable.

Well . . . except Unsu. In spite of herself, Kartek smiled. The thought of him with his emerald green eyes watching her from across the room made her heart flutter.

"There, that blush is just what you need." Oni put her hands on her hips and smiled. "You are now the perfect bride."

"The alders asked you to recreate the wedding so that the rest of the world might see and respect the union. It was always valid. This is just to make it so in the eyes of your royal peers," Cantara said as she moved Kartek's handmaidens into the proper order around her. "I still believe it was a good course of action."

"And if the idea of seeing your husband all dressed up in the kingdom's most precious jewels and wearing its sharpest weapons doesn't brighten your day," Oni gave her a sly smile, at which Kartek blushed even more, "I saw a certain young man among the guests who is most anxious to see you when this is all done."

Kartek laughed. "It's not seeing my peers that discomfits me. It's knowing that they all . . . know. What they expect *after* this."

"You mean in about six months?" Oni raised one delicate eyebrow.

"Nine," Kartek mumbled.

Oni stared at her for a moment before her eyes grew large. "You mean the night before he left, you didn't—"

"The jahira met her husband during a war, then he left for three months to settle the tribes," Cantara said, giving Oni a stern look. "I hardly think it inappropriate to give them time to reorder themselves and their peoples without distraction." But even as she finished her speech, the alder was clearly suppressing a smile.

Kartek shivered with delight and trepidation. "What if we don't have an heir? Right away, I mean. What will they assume then?" She shook her head. "I should like *that* part of marriage to be a bit more private."

"You are the jahira," Cantara said. "You are wed to the fearsome Rayis. This union is like nothing our world has ever seen before in the southern realm. Nothing you do will ever be private again." She peeked through the door. "All right. It's time."

"Don't worry," Oni whispered in her ear with an ornery grin. "I shall only give the richest of our guests tours of your bedchambers."

If Kartek hadn't been primped to perfection, she would have tried to swat her friend. Oni only laughed and danced away to her proper place at the head of the wedding train.

The change that had taken place between her first wedding and this second one was astounding, despite taking place only months apart. Where Kartek had trudged with angry solemnity down the halls the first time she was wed to Unsu, now she could find nothing in her heart except joy. Well, and nerves at being put on display in front of her most powerful allies, friends, and even a few enemies. And meeting her husband at last . . . again.

The jahira was supposed to be composed and in control at all times. Nothing should rattle her, and nothing should fill her with fear. But Kartek was not that jahira. Not yet. What if their witnesses were witness not only to the union, but to her deepest emotions, the kind of emotions that broke composure and ceremony? What if upon seeing Unsu she began to cry or freeze or something else equally as ridiculous?

In the three months since Unsu had gone to take care of his tribes, Kartek had found herself in a constant state of change. Gone was her anger at her husband, but in its place was now fear and uncertainty. Jahira was a demanding position and a lonely one, a place that Kartek had treasured but found exhausting. With the exceptions of her parents and Ahmos, Kartek had never felt the need or desire to draw someone into her innermost feelings. Even Oni, as much as Kartek loved her personal handmaiden, was never privy to Kartek's deepest thoughts, worries, and dreams. Her position was one that demanded secrecy in many ways, and Kartek had used that secrecy to shield herself from the thoughts that might bring judgment from others. But now that her reign was no longer her own . . . Now that her life was no longer her own, Kartek was very aware that her position of hiding would no longer exist. Instead, Unsu would be made aware of her faults and prejudices. He would see her shortcomings and fears. Her husband would know who she was inside and out.

She would also know the vulnerability of loving him. Kartek was not used to being vulnerable. From Ebo's skilled protection to the secrecy her position demanded, she had always been guarded in every way. But this unusual man who had traversed desert and war to protect her, had found a way into her heart. Even while he was gone, Kartek had found herself falling more and more in love with the man she had once scorned. With each day, she marveled more at the way he had studied and cared for her. Without knowing for sure that she would agree to his proposal or that she would even spare his life for making such a bold suggestion as marriage, he had risked everything to save her and her people.

If she wasn't careful to play the part of a proper jahira today, Kartek's witnesses might see just how much she loved him. And that was frightening.

The trek to the throne room seemed to take an eternity, but when they finally did reach it, she tried to use her newfound power to calm her beating heart. Since the curse had broken and she had healed Unsu from Marid's knife, Kartek had discovered a new freedom in her healing. The jewel still aided her efforts greatly, but she no longer had to fight to find the gift. It flowed from her heart easily. Calling it up was like breathing.

But it didn't help her calm down today. Apparently, she would need to leave that to the Maker.

The sounds of a crowd made her want to duck and run. She imagined her peerage watching her, judging each step and comparing it to that of her mother. But as soon as Unsu came into view, she forgot that the crowds were there at all.

His aloe green trousers and shirt were tied neatly at his waist, ankles, and shoulders, revealing smooth muscles that might as well have been carved by the Maker himself. A curved sword with a ruby-edged hilt sat on his hip, and a green jewel hung down on his forehead, mirroring hers. How had she not noticed the way the jewel brought out the green in his eyes during their first wedding? How had she missed the way his eyes saw into her soul . . . and somehow saw only the best?

When the music began this time, her step was sure as she walked toward him. A brief sideways glance at their spectators made her shudder and falter briefly, but then he was at her side kneeling before the holy man, and she found herself intoxicated by his presence again. For a fleeting second, she imagined the way it would feel if he placed his hands on her waist to steady her, but she immediately stopped herself from going any further. Too much thinking about her husband's gentle hands or soft lips, and she really would giggle. Then she would die of embarrassment.

Taking a deep breath, Kartek focused on placing her hand against his, blade against blade, sides touching. The holy man began reciting the vows. Kartek was decently sure she spoke when she was supposed to, as no one stared at her or whispered loudly to prompt her. All she could focus on was the feeling of peace that came from having this man at her side. Not just now, but as long as she lived. Their children would have a father with a gentle countenance, despite his heritage, and she would never doubt his love for any of them. *Thank you,* she thought to the Maker. *We asked for a miracle, and though I didn't deserve it, you gave.*

Somehow, in the breath of a moment, the ceremony was over. All that remained was their kiss. Even with the anxiety she had entertained about being put on display, Kartek found herself smiling ridiculously as she turned to face him.

If she had ever doubted the legitimacy of their first wedding, there was absolutely no room for fear now. Just as her power flowed from her heart through the tips of her fingers, she could now feel his passion moving through her in the warmth of his kiss. The gentle desire on his lips was sweet, and the way his hands held the nape of her neck, guiding her toward him made her feel secure in a way she hadn't felt since her parents died.

Or maybe even more so.

A few cleared throats and titters from the crowd told her that their embrace was indeed longer than the first had been, but suddenly, she didn't care. She and Unsu had nearly died in finding one another, and she deserved a moment to enjoy their success. And she was determined to take it.

Finally, the pressure of his hands lessened, but she could tell it was with great reluctance that he let her go, his green eyes filled with regret as he did. His hand didn't leave her waist.

Kartek laughed at his pathetic expression. The jahira laughed, and for once, it didn't matter who heard her.

After the ceremony was finished, Kartek and Unsu did have to part ways for a while. Between the tribal leaders, northern kings and queens, emissaries, and other important well-wishers, it was all they could manage not to offend anyone by giving any one guest less attention than any other.

And though it was with great reluctance that Kartek let go of her newly reclaimed husband, allowing him to be swallowed by the crowds, there was one guest she could at least enjoy a reunion with.

"May the Maker bless your years and make joyful your days," he said, his gray eyes staring solemnly up at hers. As always, not a golden hair was out of place, nor had he even looked in the direction of the other young people who had congregated around the food in the corner of the room. Instead, he stood straight as a pole and as serious as any adult.

Kartek drew him into a tight hug. "Thank you, Everard!" she said in his language as she pulled back just enough to study him, matching his serious expression. "It has only been a half year since I saw you last. You cannot tell me you are too old for hugs."

He watched her warily, but the corner of his mouth finally curved up. "I suppose not."

Kartek laughed and hugged him again. "How old are you now? Have you had your birthday yet?"

"I will be twelve in a month."

"I can believe it. You will be as tall as me in no time! Now how have you fared?"

Before the boy could answer, his father came to stand behind him. "He's progressing well enough. But I wish to talk of your husband, not my son."

Kartek sighed a little as young Everard immediately stiffened. Drawing the young prince out was difficult enough. She had the rebellious desire to grab the boy by the hand and run with him to the edge of the crowd, where she and Unsu might make the serious boy grin. Instead, however, she forced a stately smile and turned to face his parents.

"May your union be a blessed one, Jahira," King Rodrigue's deep baritone voice rang out as he gave her a deep nod. It was impossible not to notice how the crowd pressed outward around him, everyone doing their best to give the Destinian king his space.

"Thank you, Rodrigue," Kartek said. "I have been blessed by the Maker."

"He defeated the enchantress." The king was frowning thoughtfully at Unsu, who was talking with a southern king in the corner of the room. "I suppose he will do well enough."

"I believe you are right. How are you, Louise?" Kartek turned to Everard's mother. Had anyone else given her husband such a passing glance at his own wedding, she would have taken offense. But Kartek had learned long before that no one measured up to King Rodrigue's standards. Not even his own self. Even a glance from him was like the laud of a hundred others.

"I do not know how you survive this heat," Queen Louise dabbed at her forehead with a cotton cloth, "let alone manage to look decent."

Please, Maker, don't let her faint again. "If you need anything from my servants to make you more comfortable," Kartek said, "do not hesitate to ask."

But to her great relief, another king captured Rodrigue and Louise's attention at that moment, and Kartek turned back to Everard. "So, what do you think of my new husband?" She watched him with amusement as he stretched up on his toes to see Unsu above the crowd.

"Is he good to you?"

"What?" Kartek blinked down at him in surprise.

"Does he treat you well?"

Kartek ignored the desire to hug him again. The boy's soft lines of childhood were fast disappearing, making him look the mirror image of his father. Kartek couldn't help mourning a little as she noted that the severe angles of maturity were chasing away the remnants of childhood from his face. Though he was almost six years her junior, Kartek and Everard had found a kinship as soon as he was old enough to talk. At royal gatherings, they alone had known what it was like to be different. They were gifted and they were *other*. But so serious was the small boy and so deep were his thoughts, that Kartek had often found herself enjoying his company. Often, she wondered if being around Everard might be what it was like to have a brother.

"Does he treat you well?" Everard repeated, his eyes never leaving her face.

Kartek smiled. "Better than I deserve."

He snorted. "I doubt that."

"You know, I was not very nice to him at first." Kartek glanced around to make sure no one else was listening. "I might have even admitted to one of my servants that he looked somewhat like a frog."

Everard stared at her and then, to her surprise, gave a little laugh. "Do you think he looks like a frog now?"

"No. No, I think he looks very handsome. And brave. And kind. And good." She paused and leaned down to whisper in his ear. "Never allow your judgment to be clouded by the way people appear, Everard." She paused, watching the all-too-familiar loneliness fill the boy's eyes. "The Maker has someone for you, too."

He looked up at her, his brows furrowing. Within them, doubt warred with hope, and Kartek found herself praying that hope would one day win.

"You really care for him that much?"

"By a miracle, he has become my closest friend."

Everard drew a deep breath and nodded once, seemingly more to himself than to her. "Very well, then. I am glad you have him."

An arm wrapped itself around her waist, and Kartek smiled and leaned in as her husband's familiar form came to stand beside her.

"Emeeri Unsu," Everard bowed slightly, "you have my blessing." And with that, he turned and walked away.

Unsu looked down at her, confusion on his face. "I suppose I should be honored?"

Kartek smiled. "His approval is the highest honor I could ask for."

"He looks rather short to be a king."

"For now. But he will be a great king one day." She looked around again. To her relief, the crowds were beginning to thin. "Come." She tugged on his arm. "Let's go somewhere where we can hear ourselves think."

"I have no argument with that."

Kartek wound her way through the servants to a side door. They slipped out into a courtyard, but she led them on until they had reached the wall and escaped once again. Finally, they found the well.

"So," Unsu said, drawing her close and wrapping his arms around her, "would you have married me without this . . . future boy king's approval?"

"I think I already did." Kartek reached up to muss his hair. He tried to lean away, but she laughed and pulled herself closer. He finally managed to pin her arms to her sides and lift her in the air. Kartek laughed and squirmed, but he held her tightly against him until he was seated on a rock beneath one of the palm trees.

"Are you happy?"

Kartek stopped her teasing. Instead, she settled for leaning her head on his chest. "Of course. Why?"

"Not that I could do much about it now, but—"

"Stop right there." She placed her fingers against his lips. His eyes looked as though he had more to say, but Kartek shook her head. "We were given our places and times in this world. I lost my parents, and you lost your birthright. But the Maker has taken what was evil and made it good." She traced the shape of his jaw with her finger.

He closed his eyes and she felt him release a long breath.

"I thought I needed someone like Gahiji. But now that I've found you, I ... I can't imagine..." She drew in a steadying breath. Why was this so hard? In his absence, she had imagined this moment over and over again. But now that he was here, the words she'd planned to say were all tangled in her head. She took another breath and tried again, slowly. "Gahiji was determined to see my worth in the light of what I could provide for him. You see *me*." She shook her head. "Somehow, you always have. And then you sacrificed everything for me and my people." By accident, she met his gaze and was unable to tear her eyes from their emerald depths in the light of the setting sun. "How could I not love you?" she whispered.

"Life will be different after this." He spoke into her hair, his breath warm against her forehead. "I will be here, of course, but I will need to travel often." He shifted uncomfortably. "I have the tribes to tend to."

"Doing what?"

He frowned. "My people have a long history of violence, as do the other tribes. I would like to see what I can do to begin to change that."

She snuggled in closer and pulled his arms around her shoulders. "Nothing would make me happier."

"What it means, though, is that I will have to be gone . . . often."

Kartek tried not to let her shoulders sag the way they wanted. "I knew I was marrying the Rayis." She struggled to keep her voice even. "I knew there would be sacrifices that came with that. Only . . ." Her voice hitched. "Just be safe. Please."

In response, he lifted and turned her in his lap so she was forced to face him. A gentle smile lit his mouth as he wiped the traitorous tears from her face. "They said this union would be historical. And it will be." He drew her closer and tucked her head beneath his chin. "But not because of the politics."

"What then?" she whispered.

He leaned down for a kiss. "We're going to change the southern realm. But we're going to do it together."

"Well," she leaned for another kiss, though her heart pounded as though she were preparing to run a race, "if you're going to be leaving me anytime soon, we should probably ensure our priorities are set properly first."

He had been tracing her knuckles with his fingers, but at these words, he froze. "What do you mean?"

She tried unsuccessfully to hide her smile. "An enchantress nearly killed us both. Our people have narrowly escaped killing one another, and we have now been subjected to two weddings." She took his hand and stood, suddenly feeling shy. "Let's go to our room. I think we have earned one night of rest."

He stood and pulled her in for one more kiss, his lips lingering on hers, his breath coming just a little faster. "That sounds to me like a perfect beginning."

The Seer's Secret

Legacy of the Time Stones Trilogy, Book 1

IN ALL OF Eirin's training, there were few fighting skills she excelled at. Fortunately, evasion was one of them. When the Goblin reached for her with long, gray fingers, she sliced at its hand before ducking beneath its arm as it screeched deafeningly.

Then she took off for the nearest Citadel entrance she could see, a small door behind a hanging of ivy.

"That one got away! It's one of the students!" a Fenris trailing the Goblin shrieked. Eirin pushed her legs harder, willing them to reach the door before her pursuers did. The door had a secret sort of lock that was taught only to its inhabitants, and if she could close the door behind her before they arrived, they would be locked out.

She could hear sounds of chase behind her, not footsteps exactly, but whatever it was, it grew nearer and nearer. Even more striking than the sounds, however, was the awareness of its presence. Eirin knew exactly where her pursuer was without having to turn and look.

With one final push, she willed her legs to make it to the door. She was running so hard that she hit the door with her entire body. With no time to waste, she quickly searched until she found the lever mechanism beneath more ivy. Pressing its three parts in the correct order, she nearly wept with relief when she heard the door click open.

There was no time to rejoice, though. Whatever it was that had been chasing her caught up. With it, that strange sense of presence. Eirin still had her sword clutched in her left hand. Guided by this odd new sense, she struck out blindly at whatever it was that chased her. And by some miracle, it screamed.

Eirin turned only long enough to pull her sword free of the same Goblin she'd slashed at moments before. Rage and shock were written in its fathomless eyes as blood trickled down its shoulder. Not a death blow by any means, but Eirin took advantage of the creature's shock and shoved herself through the open door, slamming it shut and bolting it behind her. She could still hear its angry screams on the other side, but they were muffled enough that she felt safe to turn her back to the door and sprint up the stairs.

She stopped at the first window she could find and looked down over the market. By now, the people had been herded into lines. Two tall creatures with graceful pointed ears walked down the lines slowly, touching every person in turn. Alfar, Eirin quickly recalled. In days of old, they had been some of the most respected people of Solevar, before they'd all been driven mad. But her lessons had included nothing about touching people.

Why were they doing that? Better yet, where were the Sgaeth-Oir? Where was everyone?

Sounds of clanking metal from several levels up pulled Eirin's attention from the scene below, and a sickening realization replaced her questions. Her friends weren't out fighting in the market because they were fighting here.

Part of her longed to run up the stairs and join whoever was fighting there. Instinct told her that's where she needed to be. The training she'd been subjected to and the reactions she'd been conditioned to have over the years did all but yank her into the fight. And yet...

She was the worst fighter in the Citadel. There was a great chance that whoever was up there would be more endangered by her presence than helped. She could very well get whoever it was killed by accident if he or she had to come to her aid. From the sounds of the many footsteps, it was obvious that there were more than two or three warriors fighting. But what if those fighting were young ones? Some of the older children? It wouldn't be unthinkable that some of them might have wandered to the upper levels in the chaos. Surely, they wouldn't be any more endangered by her presence if they were terribly young.

Eirin wiped her sweaty palms on her tunic before gripping her sword again and charging up the stairs. Then, pausing only to listen for the direction of the fight, she burst out into the open.

Except it was no child who was fighting the four enemies in the hall. It was the Heir himself fending them off.

For a moment, Eirin couldn't help being mesmerized. Drystan had abandoned his sword and was fighting with his staff, the one with a blade on each end. His enemies were two Griffins, a White Hart, and an Imp. And each had his own inner glow, just as the Atharrachs in the market had.

They tried every sort of attack. Two at a time. Three at a time. Four at a time. Four in a row. But the staff whizzed around his body so fast that each time one tried to come near, it ended up bleeding as it jumped back to a safe distance.

The Heir was doing just fine, advancing as his enemy retreated.

Unfortunately, the careful balance of his fight was broken when one of the Griffins turned and saw Eirin.

"That one's free!" he shouted, turning and running for her. Eirin readied herself with her sword, knowing she couldn't outrun a Griffin. Even if its powerful hind legs didn't propel it forward fast enough, its golden wings could.

But Drystan was faster. As his enemies turned and ran for Eirin, he took a running start and somehow not only overtook them, but vaulted over their heads and landed in front of Eirin, plunging his staff through the Imp as he did.

"Back-to-back!" he yelled as he began once again spinning the staff. If anyone else had wanted to fight back-to-back while spinning the staff, Eirin would have immediately refused. But she'd seen Drystan fight too many times to argue. Immediately, she fell behind him, feeling his strength surge into her as she matched his movements step for step.

She may not like him, but there was a reason he had been chosen as the king's Heir at age seven.

Drystan kept them at bay, continuing to move the staff as if he had no earthly bindings to tie him down. But this couldn't continue forever. He would tire eventually. Eirin wondered how long he could last, and in her head, berated herself for endangering him of all people with her incompetence.

Honor the King. Honor the Heir. It was one of the first lessons they were taught as children. The king and his Heir were to protect the people. And the Sgaeths were to protect the king and his Heir.

Several times, one of the creatures made it around Drystan

while the others engaged him, but Eirin was ready. She struck as soon as the enemy was within reach. The Atharrach would retreat, and she would fall back into step with Drystan.

More shouting came down the hall, and to Eirin's horror, three more Atharrachs arrived. These, too, had their own glows. Two of them, a Sidhe and a Goblin, ran to jump into the fray. Instead of coming at Eirin, though, they ran for Drystan. The third stood and watched Eirin quietly. Compared to the others, she looked remarkably Human, except that her eyes were a metallic violet, reflecting the light so strongly they nearly glowed, and her dark hair glinted with a similar silver shine. Her ears had the same gentle point as the Alfar from the market had, and instead of going for Eirin, the Atharrach merely watched her with those glittering eyes. Strangest of all, though, were the lines of violet light running down the backs of her arms.

Unfortunately, Eirin was beginning to tire. Drystan seemed to be moving with as much speed and strength as ever. He'd killed three of the original group now, and showed no signs of slowing as he faced the remaining three attackers. But Eirin was not the Heir, and she was beginning to slow, her steps lagging behind his.

The Alfar removed a small, thin whip and began to unroll it. Then, with a snap of her wrist, Eirin's hands burned where the whip had wrapped itself around her wrists. The Alfar woman pulled the whip again, and Eirin's sword clattered uselessly to the floor as Eirin lurched forward toward her.

"Drystan!" Eirin screamed. Drystan had slain the last of the attacking Atharrachs, but he turned too late. The Alfar had already grabbed Eirin's hand, and her violet eyes flashed like the distant lightning Eirin had once seen through the holes in the cavern ceiling during a storm.

The woman dropped Eirin's hand as though it burned. "A Seer," she whispered, staring at Eirin as though she'd seen a dead person. "He was telling the truth!" she shouted down the hall as she began to back up. "She's a Seer! The Seer is real! Forget the Heir! They have a Seer!"

Drystan seemed frozen, a confused frown on his face as the woman continued to scream. Then he seemed to come to his senses, and two seconds later, the Alfar woman was dead at his feet.

Footsteps retreated down the hall.

"Someone else was there!" Eirin pointed for Drystan to see. "They're running away!"

"This way!" she heard a distant voice call. "Get the others. We need to get the Seer!"

But to her surprise, Drystan didn't sprint down the hall after them. Instead, he stared at her for a long moment before Eirin realized he was tilting dangerously to the side. Eirin barely had time to grab his staff so he didn't stab himself as he hit the ground.

Follow Eirin and Drystan on their journey through a land of dragons, romance, secrets, and magic in this clean young adult epic fantasy trilogy, The Legacy of the Time Stones Trilogy.

The Seer's Secret - Book 1
The Seer's Dragon - Book 2
The Seer's Sacrifice - Book 3

Dear Reader,
Thank you for journeying with me through The Green-Eyed Prince. *I*

hope you enjoyed seeing a new portrayal of the traditionally silly princess and the undesirable prince. If you want to spent more time with Unsu and Kartek, as well get free bonus content, sneak peeks at new books, discount codes, and more, join my newsletter team, Brit's Bookish Mages at BrittanyFichterFiction.com.

If you loved this story, please consider giving it a rating or review at your favorite ebook retailer or on Goodreads to help other readers find this book.

As always, thank you! Come read with me again!

ABOUT THE AUTHOR

Brittany lives with her Prince Charming, their little fairy, and their little prince in a ~~sparkling~~ (decently clean) castle in whatever kingdom the Air Force has most recently placed them. When she's not writing, Brittany can be found chasing her kids around with her DSLR and belting it in the church worship team.

Facebook: Facebook.com/BFichterFiction
Subscribe: BrittanyFichterFiction.com
Email: BrittanyFichterFiction@gmail.com
Instagram: @BrittanyFichterFiction